Gretta's Gamble

by

Marie Higgins & Stacey Haynes

Copyright © 2023 Marie Higgins & Stacey Haynes (aka Scarlett Monroe)

All rights reserved.

ISBN - **9798861621328**

PROLOGUE

"The foolish man didn't even see it coming."

Levi Montgomery sighed before lifting the glass of whiskey to his mouth, but stopping before it reached the target. He stared at the vile drink, knowing he shouldn't rely on this to help soothe his heartache, but since he had been this way for four months, it had been like an addiction, one he needed to stop quickly before it ruined his life.

He set the glass down, trying to fight the temptation. Why couldn't he forget about his woes and focus on something else? But feeling sorry for himself seemed easier than trying to be the man he once was before *she* had come into his life.

Women! They knew how to lure a man to their side and then squash him with the heel of their shoe. Falling in love wasn't worth it.

The tinkering of the piano in the saloon, and the entertainment from the dancing girls on the stage didn't divert his attention from the card game he played with his childhood friends. They had all been raised in New York City and had been as thick as thieves until reaching their adult years. That was when they went their separate ways to find employment. After ten years, they ended up back in New York, and most of them were successful in their careers.

He glanced at his friends around the card table. Eli Collier was now a co-owner of the railroad. Ryker Drummond owned several successful hotels, not only in New York, but in all the larger cities across the country. Fallon Holmes' family was in the textile business and owned factories. Harrison Holt owned a lumberyard and was constantly growing his business. Caleb Thornton... well, as far as Levi knew, the man's career was living off his family's wealth. However, from time-to-time Caleb would toil alongside their friend, Gregory Caldwell, as a detective and solving crimes.

Levi groaned softly. He had once been a confident Pinkerton agent who knew how to hunt down criminals and put them away. Now—four months later—he doubted his every move, and his gut feelings weren't as accurate. And because he had shot and almost killed *her*, he hated using his pistol. Thankfully, he hadn't lost his job yet. Of course, he couldn't stay in Colorado any longer since she lived there, which was why he made the decision to move back to New York.

In tonight's game, Caleb Thornton was winning, but Levi didn't care. There was only one thing on his mind, and hopefully, he didn't drink himself under the table thinking about his brother's misfortune.

Being Levi's older brother, Edward was certainly not the wisest. The poor sap had gotten himself engaged to Miss Penelope Lange. Edward had once held the title of *New York City's greatest catch*, but now Levi's love-struck brother would possess the title of the city's *biggest fool*. But the oldest son of the mayor had to look good and marry well. At least Levi wasn't expected to produce any heirs for his prominent family. He would leave that up to Edward and their younger sister.

"I agree with you about Edward." Ryker Drummond nodded and tossed a poker chip in the middle of the table with everyone else's bets. "No man should have to sacrifice his bachelorhood for something so demeaning."

Levi sighed. "If only my brother shared our feelings on the subject. However, as soon as he repeats his vows, his life will be ruined. I'm certain that within a year, Edward will come to regret his hasty decision."

Levi stared at his whiskey glass, wanting to take another drink, but trying his best to fight the temptation. However, he was expected at his grandmother's ball tonight, and being intoxicated was not a good thing. Most of New York City's high society would be there, and of course, Edward would announce his engagement.

But it wasn't his father Levi worried about displeasing. It was his grandmother. That woman ran the family like a strict military sergeant ran his platoon. Usually, Levi wasn't afraid of anything, but his controlling grandmother could scare ghosts.

Caleb Thornton chuckled as he collected his winnings, sliding the poker chips closer to him. "I've had my fair share of heartbreak, just as we all have, but marriage doesn't ruin every man. My three cousins found good women, and they are blissfully happy."

"That is ridiculous," Levi gasped, scowling at his friend. "Don't let your cousins fool you. Being blissfully happy—and marriage—are words that should not be used in the same sentence, let alone the same conversation."

Caleb leaned closer. "Are you saying that you will never marry?"

Levi stared into his friend's brown eyes, twinkling with humor. Caleb had gone through life being cheerful and positive, jesting over any situation. Levi couldn't blame the man for acting this way, considering the way Caleb had grown up in the *perfect* family. Unfortunately, not all people were blessed like that.

Of course, Levi's intolerance for the female species stemmed to one woman. Alexa Moore. Even now he was surprised that he had fallen for the widow in such a short time while living in Longmont, Colorado.

"Why should I marry when there is such a variation of desirable women?" Levi motioned his hand toward the dancing girls on the stage. He had to admit, there was a better selection of female attention in New York than when he lived in Colorado.

Caleb chuckled. "Montgomery, I'm just saying, that eventually we will all wed."

"Never!" Levi growled and slammed his fist on the table, bumping against the glass of whiskey. If he didn't find a way to stop the yearning for the drink soon, he would be consuming too much tonight. But there must be a way to maintain control. Liquor would certainly ruin his life if he wasn't careful.

"I'm with Montgomery," Eli Collier said, drumming his fingers on the table. "There is no reason to marry. That would only complicate our carefree lives."

"I'll drink to that." Gregory Caldwell raised his cup of whiskey before bringing it to his mouth and tossing it back. He grimaced. Clearly, this man wasn't used to drinking, either.

Ryker grinned as he dealt the cards, starting a new game. "I believe there is a solution to our dilemma. We should make a pact that none of us will ever marry. In fact, let us make a gentlemanly wager."

Caleb snorted a laugh. "Since when did we become *gentlemen*?" He pointed toward Harrison Holt and Fallon Holmes who were flirting with the dancing girls. "Our two friends certainly can't claim the title, and the rest of us... well, we aren't trying hard enough, in my opinion."

Ryker rolled his eyes. "Fine, then we'll call it a *friendly* wager."

Caleb's expression waivered slightly. "What do you have in mind?"

Ryker paused with the cards in his hand and leaned back in his chair. His gray-blue eyed gaze jumped back and forth between Caleb, Gregory, Eli, and Levi.

"Since none of us are anxious to wed," Ryker began, "I think that the first of us to succumb to marriage should forfeit something of great value."

Levi laughed loudly. "I consider my bachelorhood to be very valuable."

Caleb tossed a few poker chips on the table. "I say we make the pot even greater."

"What exactly do you have in mind, Drummond?" Eli asked.

Ryker grinned. "I have several hotels. I suppose I could wager one of those."

Gretta's Gamble

To Levi, nothing was greater than his bachelorhood. But then there was one thing he could do without. He snickered. "I have a younger sister. Can I wager Abbey?"

"Montgomery," Caleb gasped. "You cannot just go around wagering people's lives, especially not siblings."

"Fine. I won't, although it's very tempting not to." Levi folded his arms. His mind churned with ideas. Besides his bachelorhood, the only other thing of significant importance was his grandmother's pearl necklace that he was supposed to give to his bride, and since that would never happen... "I have an heirloom I can wager. It is a pearl necklace that belonged to my grandmother's grandmother. I am supposed to give it to my bride, but I will wager it to remind me to stay away from marriage."

Gregory flipped open a notepad and with his pencil, wrote down everyone's wager. "I don't have a lot of money like most of you do, but I could give up one month of my earnings."

"I love my prized steed," Caleb added. "I will wager that because that is something I never want to give up."

Eli shook his head, grinning. "To show how much I'm against the constitution of marriage, I will wager my stock in the railroad."

Ryker pointed toward Fallon and Harrison. "I know those two will join with us. I'm willing to bet that Fallon will wager money from his inheritance, and that Harrison will wager something he received after his father's death."

Levi arched an eyebrow. "If they don't, I'm certain they will have other things that are important to them." He folded his arms. The idea of wagering something his grandmother gave him was dangerous, but he was determined to win. "So, if one of us loses and has to forfeit, where does that item go?"

The men at the table grew silent. Levi realized there was one other thing that would keep him from losing... He laughed out loud. "I have the perfect answer." His friends' eyes widened. "If one of us loses, we will forfeit our item to the person who ruined our life."

Nods and verbal agreements were passed around the table.

Finally, Levi had something that would keep him from getting his heart broken again, and with this new goal in mind, he had no reason to rely on whiskey. Now, all he needed was to tell his newest Pinkerton supervisor to give him a case that would take a few months to solve. Between keeping busy with that and not wanting to lose the wager, he would certainly turn out to be the winner.

Gretta's Gamble

CHAPTER ONE

"Prepare yourself, my lady. New York's Newgate Prison is a filthy place for a noblewoman to enter."

Gretta Barrington, Countess of Brinley, sat rigid on the coach's seat, staring at the Palladian architecture style, four-story rock building from the window. Inside the coach, the temperature was nice and cozy, but once she stepped out into the weather, the late spring wind would chill her face. Of course, that was preferable to walking into that prison.

For years, stories circled about the horrid conditions and how the prisoners were treated. But in her opinion, if those people were foolish enough to get thrown in such a revolting place, they shouldn't expect to be served exquisite tea from a China cup during a social luncheon.

Gretta nodded to her uncle. "I'm very aware of how vile the place is. However, I must enter the prison to see if Charles is there. Mr. Murdock claims he found my brother in the Newgate prison, and since we paid the lawyer good money to find him, I must now do my part and see if Charles is truly alive."

Uncle Reginald sighed heavily. His weak shoulders drooped lower. "My sweet niece. I should be the one going inside instead of you."

"Nonsense." Gretta lightly tapped her fingers on her uncle's arm. If she applied more pressure, the man would surely bruise. "I cannot possibly allow you to walk in there. Not in your condition."

Uncle Reginald was dying, yet they refused to talk about it. For the man's sake, they just referred to him as being *under the weather*. In reality, his body was deteriorating rapidly, and a fly landing on his skin would make him bruise. Her physician was at a loss for how to cure Uncle Reginald's ailment.

"I shall be fine, Uncle." She gave him a reassuring smile, even if she didn't feel as brave as she tried to appear. "I'm certain the guards inside won't let anything happen to me."

"Take my pistol, just in case."

Frowning, she shook her head. Whether her uncle realized it or not, he was also losing his memory. He hadn't carried a pistol since before she married the earl a year ago. "That won't be necessary. Besides, I'm certain the prison won't allow me to carry weapons inside. I shall be fine, I assure you."

When the coach came to a stop, she scooted to the edge of the seat and waited for the coachman to open the door. She inhaled slowly through her nose, then exhaled through her mouth as she tried to calm her fiercely beating heart. It wasn't the filthy circumstances that she feared. It was seeing if the lawyer had been correct in telling her that Charles Ramsay was locked away in prison. And if indeed he was, could she get him released?

The door opened, and the driver reached out his hand for her to take as he assisted her out of the coach. Once she stood on the ground, she squared her shoulders, lifted the hood over her hair, and tightened the cloak around her shoulders. She couldn't stop staring at the menacing building looming in front of her.

I must do this. Charles would do the same for her if the roles were reversed. Then again, why would she be foolish enough to get herself thrown in a place like this? Indeed, her brother had been accused unjustly, and she would do all within her power to get him released, even if it meant selling everything that her deceased husband had purchased over the years—that he hadn't already gambled away.

She reached up to the heart-shaped ruby necklace around her neck and moved her fingers over the heart-shaped pendant. Frederick had given this to her on their first wedding anniversary. He told her the necklace had been in his family for years. She was certain it was worth a lot of money, but she didn't have the heart to sell it. However, wearing something this costly in prison was not a good idea, so she hastily removed it and placed it in her wrist purse.

As she approached the tall, iron gates, the two men standing guard gave her a quizzical look. She was certain not many women came by themselves to this type of facility, especially not a noblewoman.

"Good day," she began her greeting to the guards, but quickly cleared her scratchy throat. "I am Lady Brinley, and I have been corresponding with Mr. Murdock, my lawyer. He spoke to the warden who gave me permission to visit my brother, Charles Ramsay."

The guard nearest to her lifted his double-chin and narrowed his gaze. "Lady Brinley, are you certain you want to go inside?"

She nodded. "I thank you for your concern, but I must see my brother."

"And your brother is Charles Ramsay?" The second guard folded his slender arms behind him and rocked back and forth on his boots. "That scallywag deserves to be in prison. I wouldn't trust him as far as I could spit."

Gretta's chest tightened from his mean words. Tears stung her eyes, but she refused to cry. "Sir, it doesn't matter what you think of my brother, I must see him."

The second guard scratched his unshaven face as his gaze roamed over her attire. "I'd think a fancy lady like yourself would want to stay outside with the fresh air to breathe."

Both guards laughed heartily as if they shared a wicked secret. Gretta wouldn't give in. She knew of the prison's circumstances and was stronger than she appeared. Thankfully, her insecurities hadn't made themselves known.

"I shan't be long. Please, let me in."

The beefy guard shrugged and unlocked the gate, pulling the iron bars open for her. "The warden is just inside that door." He motioned with his head toward the entrance.

"I thank you, sirs." She nodded to both men and stepped past the gates.

The closer she came to the front double doors, the faster her heart pounded against her ribs. Her legs trembled, but she pushed forward. Turning back now would only show that she was weak, and she was far from claiming that emotion. Determination to prove herself worthy of the task guided her as she opened one of the doors and stepped inside.

Immediately, she realized the place had no heat. Perhaps having hearths in every room was impossible. Then again, it would be a way for most prisoners to escape. Now, she was grateful she wore her cloak.

She stopped in the middle of the floor as her vision adjusted to the main hall's dim lighting. From what she could tell, the stone walls were moist and moldy. A foul scent wafted through the air, and she detected urine. Shivering, she brushed off the concern even as bile rose in her throat. It was futile to think about the conditions of the prison. Her worry needed to remain on her brother.

A tall, robust man walked toward her. He wore the required uniform of the prison guards. This man looked nothing like the two she had conversed with outside only moments ago. In fact, the hearty man appeared that he could actually wrestle a bear and win.

"You must be Lady Brinley," he said, stopping in front of her. "I'm Felix Chappell. Warden Hadley told me you were coming." He shook his head. "Although, for the life of me, I don't understand why."

"Sir, it's not your place to understand. I came to visit my brother and will not leave until that has been accomplished."

His bushy eyebrows arched. "Warden Hadley warned me you were a stubborn aristocrat."

She didn't know why the warden would say such things when the man had never met her since they had only corresponded through letters. But it didn't matter. She didn't have time to argue with the guards. "Mr. Chappell, will you

Gretta's Gamble

please take me to see Charles Ramsay? It is imperative I see him today."

He bowed slightly in a mocking fashion. "If *my lady* wishes, then who am I to deny her request?"

It irritated her that these men couldn't take her seriously and seemed to mock the fact that she was from England. Why couldn't they just let her attend to her business instead of trying to talk her out of it?

This was the very reason her husband had moved them from London to live in New York City, because he couldn't stand living amongst high society. Now she wondered why the lower class treated her like a gutter rat. Who was worse? London's high society or New York's lower class? But it didn't matter. Most people who had known about Frederick's gambling issues looked down on her anyway.

The man turned and grasped a lantern from off the main desk, holding it high as he led her down a long corridor. The click from her heeled boots echoed. But then so did the voices of the prisoners crying out for freedom—or to be fed. The cells were rusted badly, proving how old the structure was.

Gretta wanted to cover her ears from the cries, but she held strong to her dignity. How any man could stand to be in this nightmarish place was beyond her. If the stench didn't make them physically ill, the voices would be what accomplished that ailment.

She dug into her wrist purse and withdrew a lacy handkerchief. She brought it up to her nose in an attempt to make the foul smell disappear. It didn't work as well as she would have liked, and she gagged.

Try as she might, she couldn't take all the sounds out of her head or the smell, but she continued to imagine her brother's face and what words of encouragement she could give him. Of course, she might cry for the first few minutes after seeing him. After all, he had been missing for a little over twelve months. Once she had received word from his landlord that rent had not been paid, she had hired a solicitor to find Charles.

For all this time, they had not heard one word. Then, Mr. Murdock received a missive from someone at the prison asking if he was still looking for Charles because a man with that description and using his name was there.

Gretta's chest tightened once again. What if it wasn't Charles? And yet it must be. There couldn't possibly be more than one man with that name.

The prison guard turned down another corridor, and the stench seemed to increase. She prayed the good Lord would help her through this miserable time in her life, not only while she was in this prison, but when she tried to free her brother.

Finally, Mr. Chappell came to a stop in front of a cell and motioned his hand toward the iron bars. "You have reached your destination, *my lady*." He looked at the person inside the cell and banged his fist on the bars. "Ramsay, get up. You have a visitor."

She didn't want to look at the other prisoners as they pressed their filthy faces against their cell bars and shouted lewd comments at her. Only one person had her interest, and it was the man in cell number twenty-six.

Gretta's whole body trembled as she stepped closer, trying to see the man in the shadows. Although the guard held the lantern, it was still difficult to see inside the small block. However, the light illuminated a man's shoulder-length, matted hair. How long had he been in prison? She prayed it wasn't very long at all.

The unrecognizable man stumbled as he slowly stepped toward her. His hunched-over position made her wonder if he was disfigured for a reason or if it was due to the small cells. After all, her brother was tall.

With each step he took toward her, she was able to see a little more. His clothes were ragged. Obviously, he had been in this place for too long. The dirt on his face made it difficult to see his identity, and she couldn't see his eye color because of the shadows.

His long fingers on one hand wrapped around the rusted bars, and he pulled himself upright a little taller. Still, she

Gretta's Gamble

couldn't tell if this was Charles or not, mainly because his gaze narrowed on her as if seeing her for the first time.

"Charles? Is that really you?" Her voice cracked as she spoke.

"Gretta?" He paused briefly and shook his head. "No, that cannot be you. I must be dreaming."

Although her brother had been missing since right after Frederick died a year ago, wouldn't she remember his voice? This man's voice didn't sound like Charles', instead, it was too strained.

She tightened her fingers around her handkerchief, still keeping it to her nose. "If you are my brother, tell me something only he would know about me."

"Oh, don't do this to me," he muttered. "I *am* your older brother."

She shook her head. "Tell me, or I'm leaving."

"When we were children, we lived in Devonshire."

"No. That isn't something only you would know about me. Anyone can obtain that information."

His wide chest rose and fell slowly as a deep breath expelled from him. "You had a cat named Brandy."

Irritation filled her, and she pursed her lips. "I'll give you one more chance before I turn around and leave this place as quickly as I entered."

"But you did have a cat—"

"And if you were one of our neighbors or a relative, you would know that."

"Will everyone know that you named the cat Brandy because of the way the sun hit her fur?"

Not fully convinced, Gretta took a step back. His other hand grasped the bars.

"And does everyone know that you hid the cat in your armoire during our mother's social luncheons because she hated that the feline always strolled through the parties and jumped on the tables? And before you say any more," he continued without taking a breath, "nobody knew that about the cat except your family because Ma would have been devastated if society knew that Brandy was our best-kept secret."

Tears filled Gretta's eyes as her throat tightened with relief and happiness. "Charles, I finally found you." She moved to the bars and touched his fingers, pressing her forehead against the rusted steel, but she didn't care.

"Oh, my dearest Gretty." His voice broke as he awkwardly kissed her fingers. "I never thought—"

Gretta jumped back as if she had just been thrown into the Hudson River during the winter. She clutched her hands against her chest. Anger filled her, and her tears quickly disappeared. "Who are you? Because you certainly are *not* my brother."

"Are you insane? Of course, I'm your brother." He shook his head.

"Charles has *never* called me Gretty."

The man's eyes widened. The light from the lantern highlighted the eye color, and her heart sank. The man in the cell even had different eyes. Although this man had blue eyes, Charles' were grayish blue like hers.

The tightness in her chest continued, making it difficult to breathe. Although she wanted to cry because this wasn't her brother, she wanted to yell at him for trying to trick her. Why would this stranger want to play with her emotions in such a way? And pray, why did Mr. Murdock make her believe the prisoner was her brother?

As much as she wanted to spin around and run out of the wretched place as fast as her feet could carry her, she wanted answers more. This man knew her, but how? Could he have known Charles, and if so, could he tell her where to find her brother?

CHAPTER TWO

Levi Montgomery stared at the lovely countess, silently berating himself for the untimely slip-up. Charles had once mentioned that he gave his sister a nickname, and naturally, Levi assumed it was Gretty. Sadly, this fact hadn't presented itself *after* he convinced her to pay for his freedom. But the mistake had been made, and he must try to set things right the best he could.

"Gretta, please—"

Lady Brinley threw him a glare. "Do not be so informal with my name, sir."

She stepped back, appearing as if she was ready to flee. He couldn't allow her to leave yet. "No, wait."

Keeping her shoulders stiff and chin erect, she kept her steely gaze on him. "Give me one good reason why I should stay. After all, you are not the man you proclaim to be."

Levi couldn't possibly tell her why he was really in this jail cell pretending to be her brother. So, for now, he would create a believable story, using only a few facts to back him up.

"Lady Brinley, I want to find Charles, as well. If we work together, I know we could find him. I believe he is in danger." His knees ached from the cramped, dank environment, so he adjusted his stance. He couldn't be in the small cell any longer than necessary.

Even in the shadows, he noticed that her face had lost color. Maybe he shouldn't have sprung the *danger* topic on her already.

Her throat jumped as if she swallowed hard. "Is he truly in danger?"

"I think he is, which is why we need to find him quickly."

"We? Why do you presume I want to work with you when I have a solicitor?"

Levi decided to add a touch of sympathy to his voice. "I want to find Charles just as you do. He was my friend before disappearing. Perhaps the only way to find him is by combining our knowledge and memories of the man."

As much as Levi wanted to convince her that she needed him, the truth was, he needed her. He could never complete his assignment without Lady Brinley. The lovely widow would help him find the heirloom belonging to the wealthy Mrs. Kensington from New York, especially since Lady Brinley's brother had stolen it before disappearing.

As Levi studied her, he could now see the resemblance she shared with her brother. From what he could see of her hair, it appeared black, but then he couldn't be certain since the lighting in the prison was terrible and she still wore a hood. More than likely, her hair color was probably similar to Charles's, which was dark brown. If Gretta had the same color of eyes as her brother, they would be grayish-blue.

Normally, men didn't remember particular traits in people, but Levi had been a Pinkerton agent for five years, and because he had been well-trained, he suspected Charles was in disguise by now. Six months ago, Levi had met Charles Ramsay at a poker game. As one of Levi's jewelry theft suspects, he made certain to keep the man drinking—and talking—which is where he learned so much about Gretta Barrington, the Countess of Brinley, who had moved to New York City from England.

Another thing Levi knew was that Charles had been in a fight and had gotten a cut on his chin. Thankfully, facial scars were harder to hide. Nevertheless, looking for the man would be more difficult, which is why he knew that if he convinced the man's sister to help him, Levi would actually be able to capture the thief.

This case had been going on too long, and Allan Pinkerton wanted results. Levi couldn't blame his employer since Mrs. Kensington had been waiting over a year already for her family heirloom to be returned. The case had grown cold six months ago, but then it was assigned to Levi. He was determined to bring closure to this case one way or another—even it meant suffering in this dank cell for a few minutes longer.

Slowly, Lady Brinley's harsh expression relaxed, and tears filled her eyes again. He truly didn't want to lead her astray, but his assignment was important. Justice needed to be served, and Levi was the Pinkerton agent to do it.

She stepped closer. "Who are you, and when did you meet my brother?"

"I'm Levi Montgomery, and I met Charles Ramsay just over a year ago while at the gaming tables in New York City."

"Was Charles your friend?" she asked with a shaky voice.

He nodded. "We were as close as brothers." It pained him to speak of Ramsay in the past tense only because Levi had learned a hard lesson from lying to women. Yet he also learned that most people couldn't be trusted.

A tear slid down her face. "Why are you in prison?"

Sighing, he relaxed his hands grasping the bars and began the untrue story. "I lost a card game and I owe money to a prominent citizen in the city. Because I couldn't pay the debt, he had me thrown in this vile place." It was a plausible reason, especially since that was the story he had heard from many men in here.

"How much money do you owe?"

Levi pointed toward Felix Chappell, who happened to also be a Pinkerton agent. "That man who brought you to me will know all the details."

Both Levi and Felix had worked together several times since Levi's arrival in New York. Felix worked undercover as a prison guard whenever the occasion arose, which was helpful for when Levi needed to collect information on criminals. Surprisingly, he and Felix found most of their suspects in prison.

She turned and stepped toward Chappell. Levi prayed this would work. It had to. This was the only way to get close to Lady Brinley. Both he and Chappell had been working on this assignment for six months now. Sadly, Levi didn't know what happened to Charles, but since the man was a thief, prison was in the man's future. Still, Levi wanted to capture the man and confiscate Mrs. Kensington's expensive heirloom.

Felix Chappell talked in a hushed voice with Lady Brinley, but then they moved back toward Levi's cell. Chappell leaned against the bars, looking at Levi.

"The lady here says she wants to pay your debt."

Levi didn't dare sigh with relief yet. Not until he walked out of prison today. "And what is the hold-up, sir?"

"The lady has stipulations."

Levi shifted his gaze to Lady Brinley. "What stipulations?"

She kept a straight back and an erect chin. "Mr. Montgomery, I will pay your debt, but you must return my generosity by working for me until the payment has been met."

He hitched a surprised breath. *Work for her?* Excitement jumped inside him. Her suggestion was an even better plan than the one he had devised.

"I will accept the deal," he quickly said. "What will you have me do while under your employ, my lady?"

"I am in need of someone to work in my stable."

He didn't mind working outside, especially since most of his assignments had him outdoors anyway. At least he would be closer to her and watch her every day. "I can do that as well as look for your brother."

Levi watched her expressions change from wary to hopeful, then to determined. She nodded and opened her wrist purse. As she poked her fingers inside, she appeared to be searching for something in particular.

He held his breath, wondering if she was carrying the necklace her brother had stolen from the old widow. After all, Charles had mentioned that one time while in a drunken state, that his brother-in-law had gambled away most of their money. Levi figured she would want to pay his debt by using jewelry, and with any luck, it would be Mrs. Kensington's necklace.

Finally, she withdrew some banknotes. Inwardly, he groaned. So, she didn't pay with jewelry, but he would find it in her home soon.

Gretta's Gamble

Lady Brinley turned to Chappell, handing him the money. "This should cover Mr. Montgomery's debt."

Levi's friend counted the notes before giving the countess a nod. "Yes, these will cover everything."

"Splendid. Now, will you please release Mr. Montgomery into my custody?"

Chappell stepped to the gate and withdrew some keys. He met Levi's gaze and grinned. Thankfully, Lady Brinley couldn't see the look of victory on Chappell's face at this moment. She would certainly suspect the so-called guard and Montgomery were up to some tomfoolery.

As they all walked toward the front part of the prison, the other prisoners banged on the bars of their cells, displaying their anger and frustration in high-pitched voices. Some of them wiggled their arms from between the bars, begging for Lady Brinley to assist them with their debts, but her quick step didn't falter as she kept her attention focused ahead.

Chappell opened the front doors of the prison, and Levi hurried outside. Fresh air hit him like a bucket of cold water, and he breathed in the pleasant scents. He had to admit that pretending to be a prisoner had been difficult. The stench was unbearable.

Lady Brinley didn't look back at him but continued to head toward the fancy coach parked across the street. As she neared the vehicle, her coachman jumped down and opened the door. The confusion on the man's face stayed on Levi as he followed the lady.

"Gilbert?" She looked up at the driver who turned his head and met her stare. "This is Mr. Montgomery." She motioned with her hand toward Levi. "He is in my employ now, and he will ride up with you until we reach the house."

The driver's eyes widened, and his mouth dropped open, but just as quickly, he closed it and blinked several times.

"Are you sure, Lady Brinley?"

"Yes, Gilbert."

Levi moved his gaze into the luxurious coach with the silky cream-colored walls, the cushioned benches, and… He sucked in a fast breath. There was a dead man in the vehicle.

Immediately, his instincts took over, and he jumped into action, moving in front of the countess and entering the coach. She shrieked and instructed her coachman to stop Levi, but his focus was on the dead man… or at least the man inside who appeared dead.

The older gentleman's head was tilted back in a crooked position as it rested against the wall, and his mouth hung agape. But it was the grayish tint of the man's skin that worried Levi.

He pressed his fingers against the man's neck, trying to feel the pulse from his heartbeat, but nothing was detected. In a flash, Levi laid the man on the seat and pressed on his chest three times.

"What are you doing?" Lady Brinley shrieked. "You are going to bruise him."

"Lady Brinley," he said without looking at her since the old man deserved some attention first. "I'm trying to save his life. He isn't breathing."

"Oh, dear." Her voice tightened. "Please be careful. He is very feeble."

Levi pressed his fingers against the man's neck again. Still nothing.

Not often did he try and save someone's life this way, there was one other thing he could try. His grandfather, a physician, breathed into a dying woman's mouth, and it caused her to breathe on her own. Levi would try it. At this point, this was his last resort.

Being as careful as he could, he placed his mouth over the older man's mouth and blew. Immediately, the man gasped and blinked open his eyes. The moment the man realized what might have happened, he pushed Levi away.

"I beg your pardon, sir." The man grumbled and struggled to sit up. "How dare you take such liberties—"

"Uncle Reginald," Lady Brinley called out as she climbed inside the vehicle. "This man just saved your life." Tears coated her eyelashes, and she gently touched the older man's arm. "You had stopped breathing."

"Impossible." He lifted his chin stubbornly. "I was merely sleeping deeply."

"*Very* deeply," Levi said. "Because I could not feel your heartbeat."

The elderly man's gaze ran over Levi from the top of his matted hair down to his very worn boots. The man's lip curled in disgust.

"Who are you, and what are you doing in my coach?"

"Uncle," Lady Brinley said again, but her voice wasn't tightened with emotion this time. "This man is from the prison. I paid for his release, and he will work for me."

"What?" The uncle's voice lifted as he stared wide-eyed at his niece. "Have you lost leave of all your senses?"

"Uncle, please." She shook her head before turning to Levi. "I thank you for your assistance, but if you don't mind, we need to get my uncle home now. You can ride up top with Gilbert."

Disappointment filled Levi, even though it shouldn't, considering his disguise. "I understand." He exited the coach and climbed up to sit beside the driver. Of course, the servant called Gilbert, gave Levi the same disapproving glare as Uncle Reginald had.

For now, Levi would brush off the judgmental stare. If roles were reversed, he would do the same to the man who had been in prison. But most definitely, these uppity people would see a new man very soon.

CHAPTER THREE

Gretta paced the hall in front of Uncle Reginald's bedchambers, nibbling on the tip of her thumbnail. Once they had reached home, she summoned her uncle's physician. The incident inside the coach scared her half to death. Of course, she knew her uncle was dying, but she didn't want him to leave this world yet. She needed his company desperately. Having the elderly man around made her feel important and needed. Since Charles's disappearance, that was something she greatly craved.

For a moment earlier outside the prison, when Mr. Montgomery had jumped into the coach, she wondered if the man was trying to steal something. But then she glimpsed her uncle's skin, and most certainly, the man hadn't been breathing.

During the ride home, Uncle Reginald seemed disoriented, which worried her much more. Perhaps it was time to hire someone to be with him constantly to make certain he didn't stop breathing, but that was impossible since the person she hired would have to sleep, too.

The door to Uncle Reginald's bedchambers opened, and the doctor stepped out, carrying his black leather medical bag. She stopped pacing and faced the middle-aged man with brown hair dusted with gray around the ears and forehead.

"How is he?" she asked, wringing her hands.

He shrugged. "He is about the same as when I last checked on him two days ago." He stepped closer and patted her shoulder. "Lady Brinley, I understand your fear of him dying, but we cannot stop it. If it's his turn to meet the Lord, we must let it happen."

Sadness clogged her throat, making it difficult to swallow. "I know, but... I don't think it's his turn to die."

"Well, your uncle was most fortunate this time, and the servant that acted so hastily did indeed save Lord Reynold's life."

She blinked back the tears stinging her eyes. "My new servant is very skilled, I must say. I have never seen that maneuver done before."

"I'm most interested to learn that technique as well."

The physician stepped in the direction of the front door since Uncle Reginald's room was on the main level to keep him away from the stairs. She didn't want anything causing him harm.

"I shall speak to my servant and inform him to teach you what he knows." She smiled through trembling lips.

"I would appreciate it." He nodded. "Please call on me again if you have any more worries."

"I shall."

She walked him to the door and waited for him to leave before hurrying back to her uncle's bedchamber. Slowly, she opened the door and peeked toward the bed where she knew the man would be. Her uncle was propped up with several pillows behind him as a quilt covered him from his waist to his legs. He wore a nightshirt as though he was ready for bed, holding a book and reading.

Gretta sighed and leaned against the doorframe. She couldn't keep an eye on him all the time. It just wasn't done. All she could do was pray that it wasn't his time to meet the Lord.

She pulled away and quietly closed the door. With a heavy heart, she took slow steps toward the dining room. It wasn't quite time for supper, and honestly, she wasn't really hungry. She had the most stressful day, and all she wanted to do was retire for the evening.

On the way home from the prison, she had argued with her uncle about the new man she had hired. Even as she explained to her uncle that Mr. Montgomery was a friend of Charles's and would help her look for her brother, she felt the words were meaningless. Several times during the heated conversation, she thought about turning the vehicle around and putting him back in prison. However, she had paid his debt with money her uncle had given her, and now the man owed her money. Having him work for her was the only way to get it back. She hoped he wouldn't run off before the debt was paid.

She would be on guard, watching him. After all, he wasn't an honest man. Yet seeing him care for her uncle had softened her heart. Mr. Montgomery couldn't be such a terrible person if he made an effort to save a stranger's life. Could he?

Sadly, her head continued to argue with her heart over this matter. She feared she had put too much trust in the thief. However, he was Charles's friend. In the end, she couldn't abandon Mr. Montgomery. Not yet, anyway.

Instead of ending in the dining room, which was where she had headed, she found herself outside. The weather had cooled quite a bit, but she didn't want to return to the house to fetch her shawl or her bonnet.

Her feet must have had minds of their own because she walked toward the stable. She should speak with Mr. Montgomery since she hadn't found a moment to do so since she arrived home. Her mind had been occupied by her uncle, but now it was time to set some rules for her new servant.

As she approached the stable, one of the side doors was ajar. The closer she came, the more she heard the soothing tone of a man's voice as he hummed a tune she hadn't heard since childhood.

Gretta stopped at the door and peeked inside, searching for the baritone voice. A man stood with his back toward her near a horse as he brushed the animal's mane. She didn't recognize him as one of her stable hands, mainly because he was taller and his hair was longer, which was probably why he had pulled the dark brown bulk away from his face and gathered it in a leather band. His clothes were that of a farmer, and his knee boots fit his calves well. However, it was the sound of his voice that made her curious. Why did she feel as if she had heard it before?

She should march up to him and demand he leave. Trespassers on her property would not be tolerated. But when she opened the door wider and stepped inside, he turned and looked at her. Familiarity hit her like a bucket of icy river water.

"Mr. Montgomery?" she asked, still unsure about her obvious distorted vision.

He nodded. "Lady Brinley."

Gretta ran her gaze over him again, admiring his wide shoulders and how his shirt practically stretched across his muscular chest. He was also clean-shaven, and it surprised her how handsome he was underneath all the dirt and facial hair he had while in prison.

"Pardon me for not knowing what to say," she began slowly, "but I fear you look nothing like I had expected."

Chuckling, he turned back to the horse and continued to brush the animal. "I prefer this look compared to the one I had when we first met." He shrugged. "But the guards didn't feel it necessary to give us soap and water, especially, not a razor for shaving."

She swallowed hard, hoping to moisten her suddenly dry throat. "That is understandable." She licked her parched lips. "But I'm glad it's you and not a trespasser."

He stopped brushing and turned toward her again. "Did you wish to speak with me about something?"

"I do." She stepped closer, clutching her hands together. "I want to first thank you for what you did to help my uncle. His health is poor, but I didn't think he would stop breathing while waiting for me in the coach." She took a deep breath. "I'm truly amazed at the technique you used to make my uncle breathe."

"My grandfather was a physician, and I saw him use this on someone who was dying. I didn't know if it would work or not, but the idea came to me quickly, so I went with it."

"Well, Mr. Montgomery, your instincts were correct." She smiled. "And Doctor Fairbanks requests that you show him how to do it."

Mr. Montgomery lifted his eyebrows and nodded. "I would be very happy to."

She stepped closer, stopping on the other side of the horse. She touched the animal's mane. "I also thought I would come to talk to you about the rules I expect my servants to follow."

"Yes, of course." He stopped brushing, and his gaze stayed on her. "But before you do, may I ask after your uncle's welfare?"

Her heart lightened. "He is sitting up in bed reading. The doctor told me he is fine now, but..." She sighed heavily. "He is dying. I know it, but it doesn't make it any easier to handle."

"Do you have someone caring for him on a daily basis?"

She shook her head. "Uncle Reginald refuses help. He doesn't want people to worry over him constantly."

"That is understandable."

"But I thank you for inquiring after him." She smiled.

"I'm just sad we met in such an awkward situation."

Recalling how it happened, she chuckled. "Yes. I'm certain it's a moment my uncle will never forget. Me, either, for that matter."

Mr. Montgomery's mouth stretched into a grin. "Well, whenever you need a bit of entertainment, you know who to ask."

"Indeed, I do." She shifted from one foot to the other. Not that she was uncomfortable around him, but she was thrown off guard by his handsome appearance. "Now, about the rules."

"Go ahead. I'll listen while I finish brushing the horse."

As she watched him care for the animal, she realized he had the same compassion for people. After all, he acted immediately when he had noticed Uncle Reginald wasn't breathing. So, perhaps she shouldn't keep Mr. Montgomery in the stable. The man would better serve her working in the house and near her uncle.

"I just had a thought." She moved to the bucket of carrots and pulled one out for the horse. As she fed the animal, she tried not to peer directly at Mr. Montgomery. "I previously told you that you would work inside the stable, but I have changed my mind."

His hand stopped midway in brushing, and his gaze jumped up to meet hers. "You have?"

"Instead, I would like you to work inside the house as my…" Her mind scrambled to find the position he would best fit with. "As my footman."

He grinned. "I've never been anyone's footman before."

"My butler will teach you. His name is Conrad."

"I must admit that although I love horses, I love people more."

She laughed. "As do most of us. And you shall live in the house with the other servants instead of outside in the stable."

"I find I love my new position even more now."

She enjoyed his good humor. "Splendid. I'm going to add something more to your footman duties. I would also like you to keep an eye on Uncle Reginald. If he stops breathing again, you are the only one who can revive him."

"I can do that. As long as he isn't already dead, I shall help him to start breathing again."

Relief flooded her, and she wanted to jump with happiness. She also wanted to hug this very handsome man, but *that* she would not do.

"Mr. Montgomery, you will take your meals with the other servants downstairs in their common room, but Conrad can show you around that section of the house."

"Lady Brinley, you are such a sweet person. I have never had an employer as kind or as pretty."

Heat rushed to her cheeks. *Goodness!* Why did he have to say that? It was different that she thought him handsome, but she would never speak it aloud. Yet he was free with the compliment, and now she worried he wouldn't know how to speak properly while around her family and friends. Hopefully, he would learn to curb his thoughts and not say them aloud.

"Uh, I thank you for that compliment, Mr. Montgomery. However, that is not the correct thing to say to your employer."

"Forgive me. I didn't mean to offend. I was just expressing my thoughts." He moved closer to her. "Because I'm not used to working for someone so lovely, I wanted to let you know that."

Her heartbeat quickened. "Yes, well… in the future, while under my employ, you shouldn't say such things."

"Then, Lady Brinley, would it be too much for me to ask if you could give me etiquette lessons? After all, I'll be in a higher position and want to ensure I do my job correctly."

Cotton had somehow taken up residency in her throat, making it difficult to swallow. Images of her instructing him in the correct decorum passed through her mind, and once again, her face filled with heat. In fact, her whole body had grown very warm.

She should *not* imagine things like that. Perhaps appointing him as her footman wasn't a good idea at all.

CHAPTER FOUR

Levi tried not to grin too wide. His plans were turning out better than he had hoped. *A footman?* He would have been satisfied in the stable, but her idea was much better. Although he had never held a footman's position, his family hobnobbed with wealthier people and Levi was able to see what the servants did. But it would certainly be something he had never done while working undercover as a Pinkerton agent. After the case was finished, he would be able to mark off that particular skill.

He met the butler first thing the next morning. Conrad was a rather short man, in Levi's opinion. Perhaps being tall wasn't a requirement for a butler. At least Levi knew that if the countess needed something that she couldn't reach, she would ask him to get it for her.

The short, stout man appeared to be in his early forties. His brown hair showed signs of graying, and his solemn expression displayed wrinkles on his forehead and around his eyes. Levi wondered if the man smiled or laughed at all. Having a serious butler all the time just would not do. Levi vowed to make the man smile during the time he played footman. What good was living if one could not laugh daily?

After Conrad had shown Levi where he would be sleeping, the butler proceeded to give him the tour of the manor. He noticed many pricy artifacts and some that were not so costly, but what confused him was the rumors he had heard about the viscount's gambling habit and how he had been in debt before his death. Although the manor didn't prove that theory, the lack of servants certainly showed that the countess was indeed down on her luck.

The morning passed quickly without Levi seeing Gretta. Conrad informed Levi that the countess and her uncle took their morning meal in their rooms. It frustrated Levi only because he wanted to discuss Gretta's missing brother and what they could do to find him. However, that task was put on hold. Conrad had him cooped up in rooms most of the time, polishing the silver and trimming the lamps.

In the early afternoon, Levi accompanied the cook and one of the maids into town. Lady Brinley had requested a special menu for tonight's meal. Her uncle was eating better, and since this particular meal was to please him, the countess wished him to be happy with some of his favorite foods.

At first, Levi thought this would be a good chance to ask the kitchen staff about Charles Ramsay in hopes of collecting more information. But when he was instructed to ride on top of the carriage with the driver, it irritated Levi. He was finally in a good position to find out more about Charles, and yet Levi couldn't ask anyone. This just would not do. He just needed to figure out how to change the situation.

He glanced at the driver, trying to remember his name. Oh yes, Gilbert. Levi cleared his throat. "I hope you don't mind me asking, but how long have you worked for the countess?"

The man was probably in his late thirties, but his leathery face let Levi know that the man spent more time outside than indoors.

"Three years."

"So, I assume you know the countess well."

"Well enough."

Levi rolled his eyes. The man would talk his ear off if he didn't stop him. "Did you ever meet her brother, Charles?"

"No."

Levi shook his head, realizing he had better shut the man off before he said something out of turn. Perhaps the driver was the wrong person to get information from.

Once they reached town, Levi hurried after the kitchen maids as they rushed from shop to shop, collecting the things needed for the meal. He had tried a few times to chat with them, but they didn't have time for conversation. Mainly because they yacked with each other and didn't include him.

Upon returning home, he carried the packages into the kitchen. Mrs. Patterson was a tall woman who reminded him of his mother. The white-haired cook was full of smiles, except when she scolded the kitchen maids for ogling Levi and giggling like schoolgirls whenever he was around.

"Mrs. Patterson?" Levi asked after the maids had left the kitchen.

The older woman took her apron off the hook on the wall and wrapped it around her middle. "Yes, Mr. Montgomery."

"How long have you worked for the countess?"

She leaned against the cutting table in the middle of the kitchen and gazed toward the window as if deep in thought.

"Oh, if I have to count the years, I fear I'll forget a few." She chuckled and turned back to her task of unwrapping the packages. "You see, I have worked for the Brinley family since before we left London. I suppose it's been six years now. When I was young, my mother was the cook for Lord Frederick's parents."

"How long have you known the countess?"

She glanced at Levi and arched an eyebrow. "Our current mistress?"

Levi nodded. "Yes, of course."

"Lady Brinley has been a wonderful employer, but since the death of her husband and her brother's disappearance, the light in her eyes has dimmed. I never met her until after she married, and Lord Brinley brought her to live in New York City."

"Can you tell me how her husband died?"

The cook withdrew a large knife from the cutting block and whacked it against the meat as she cut the pork into pieces. "The poor man." She shook her head. "Lord Brinley was found dead in a field." She paused as tears filled her eyes. "Nobody knew what happened or how he was shot in the chest."

Confusion filled Levi, but he dared not speak his mind. How could a nobleman get shot in a field, yet nothing had been reported to the New York Police Department for further investigation? There were only a few times in his career when someone of importance—or a titled lord—had been killed. He would have recalled hearing about this one, especially since the man was in the field.

Levi held his breath as an idea struck him. Had the Earl of Brinley been dueling? Things like that only happened in England anymore, but if that were the case, nobody would report it because dueling was illegal. There were really only two reasons for titled lords to duel. They either disagreed at the gaming tables, or one man was defending his family's honor. *An affair?* Did Lord Brinley have an affair and was called out because of it? Hopefully, Levi would discover the truth soon.

"How odd," Levi muttered.

"Odd, sir?" The cook glanced at him again.

"Indeed. I'm surprised the police didn't have the death investigated further. After all, an earl was killed."

Mrs. Patterson shrugged. "I believe Lady Brinley tried to find answers, but when her brother disappeared soon afterward, all of her focus went into finding him."

Levi scratched his neck. "What do you know about her brother?"

The cook placed the knife on the cutting table and turned toward Levi. She opened her mouth to speak but stopped, and her gaze shifted to a point behind him. Her eyes widened, and Levi heard someone clearing their throat loudly.

He swung toward the person who had entered the kitchen. The butler's menacing expression was aimed at Levi.

"I believe, Mr. Montgomery," Conrad said stiffly, "if all you have time for is tittle-tattle, then I have not given you enough to do."

Levi groaned. The butler had chosen the wrong time to interrupt.

"And you, Mrs. Patterson, should not be spreading gossip." Conrad motioned with his arm toward the door. "Mr. Montgomery, if you will come with me, it is time for Lady Brinley's tea, and she will not be happy if we are late."

Gretta's Gamble

Grumbling under his breath, Levi followed the butler out of the kitchen. They passed the maids putting together some bite-sized cakes on a tray. He gave them a nod, and they giggled profoundly.

He tried not to encourage them any further by smiling, but it was difficult to ignore the boost of confidence it gave him from their reaction. If he wasn't trying to charm them and they acted this way, what would the result be when he sought to charm Gretta? She was obviously more mature, but he needed to get her to open up to him. How else would they find her missing brother?

"Lady Brinley requires her tea at precisely three o'clock." Conrad stopped in the room with wall-to-wall dishes. He pointed toward the several sets of cups and matching teapots. "She uses the gold-rimmed floral design on Wednesdays."

Levi arched an eyebrow. "Only on Wednesday? Why is that, I wonder?"

The butler's scowl deepened. "We are not here to ask questions. We are only here to comply with her wishes."

Deciding to shut his mouth and do as was instructed, Levi listened to Conrad explain how to set up the tea service for the countess. He had to admit, he hadn't realized until now all that had gone into being a footman. The English certainly had their odd ways that was vastly different than the first-class aristocrats here in the United States. Nevertheless, one thing remained the same—the butler ran the household with help from the housekeeper. In this case, it was Conrad who watched with eagle-eyes.

Levi shook his head. That butler needed to lighten up a bit. By the way the man acted, he would have been better-suited working as a prison warden than inside a manor. Levi didn't have a good feeling about the butler but didn't know why. It was probably because the man was constantly keeping his eyes on Levi.

Once everything was placed on the silver tray, he carefully carried it toward the sitting room where the countess would be waiting. He wanted to remind the butler that it wasn't three o'clock yet. In fact, he still had five minutes before he was considered late.

The dishes rattled on the tray as Levi walked, and Conrad followed, clearing his throat loudly. Either the butler was feeling ill, or he was hinting not-so-subtly that Levi hold the tray more steady.

What would the middle-aged man do if Levi suddenly dropped the tea service? He imagined the man would give him a proper scolding after picking himself off the floor from having heart palpitations.

Perhaps it was time to shake the man up just a bit. There was no reason to act as if he was a dog that followed commands.

The parlor was just on the other side of the staircase. This place would be the perfect spot to pretend to stumble.

Levi held back a grin as he purposely tripped. The tea service shook on the tray, even though he wouldn't let anything happen to the countess' precious dishes.

"Mr. Montgomery," Conrad cried out and jumped toward Levi, reaching out to grab the tray.

At that moment, there was a movement on the stairs. Levi glanced just in time to see Gretta tilting as if she was going to plunder down the three steps to the bottom floor.

Immediately, he reached for her, not caring about the tray in his hands. Catching her from falling was more important.

Just as the dishes crashed to the floor, shattering into many pieces, he wrapped his arms around the countess before she landed on top of the broken tea service. At first, her pale skin and wide eyes worried him, but at least he kept her from getting cut by the debris on the floor.

Confusion filled her expression, followed by her cheeks blooming with a sudden burst of color when she realized how intimately he held her against his chest. Seconds later, her face changed to panic and then to anger.

"What have you done?" she screamed at him, pushing him away as she stepped back.

Gretta's Gamble

He could see she had twisted her ankle, and although he reached out to steady her, she slapped his hands away as she peered at the broken dishes and the spilled tea.

"Forgive me, Lady Brinley, I—"

"Don't you know…" She shook her head. "That was my favorite…" Tears glistened in her eyes before she turned toward him and hit his chest. "That belonged to my mother."

He sighed heavily and pushed his fingers through his hair. He hadn't meant to do any of this, so how could it have spiraled out of control so fast? He especially hadn't planned on upsetting her to where she wanted to cry.

"I beg your forgiveness, my lady," he said humbly.

"Lady Brinley," Conrad said, rushing to her and taking her arm. "You need to sit in the parlor. Montgomery and I will clean this mess. I'll have another tea brought to you."

"I don't care about more tea." She glared at Conrad before switching her accusing focus to Levi. "This will come out of your pay."

"Yes, of course," he muttered.

It broke Levi's heart to see her spirit as shattered as the dishes. Perhaps playing around just to get the butler to loosen up hadn't been a wise decision after all.

* * * *

Gretta sat on the sofa in silence as she stared at the hearth but didn't see anything. Her heart was in turmoil, and she couldn't take any more misfortune. Nothing in her life had gone as planned. When would she finally be at peace and live a normal life? Then again, what was normal? Conflict and heartache seemed to be with her all the time.

First, it started when she discovered her father had signed the betrothal papers for her marriage to Frederick Barrington. Although she generally liked the man, she wasn't in love with him. It hadn't mattered that he was an earl. She wanted what most girls wished for when they were young. *Love.*

Sadly, Frederick never gave her that. She didn't know why he had offered marriage if he didn't want to get to know his wife and fall in love. Instead, he spent more time with his friends hunting or at the gaming tables. And who knew what other sport he had that she hadn't discovered?

When he was found dead in the field, she wasn't certain if the news made her happy or sad. Society had dictated that she mourn for a man she didn't love for a whole year, which she did, but most of the time, she did what she had always done. She had become accustomed to riding alone or making friends with the servants.

As soon as she heard about her brother's disappearance, she was grateful for something different to do so she wouldn't have to act like the grieving widow any longer. Yet the more she heard about her brother's life, the more she feared he was truly in danger. Or perhaps he was already dead by now.

Gretta groaned and rubbed her forehead. There was a slight pound in her skull from what happened an hour ago with the tea service. It still upset her that her new servant had dropped the dishes. However, now her mind tried to reason that he was just trying to save her from falling down the stairs. He didn't know that she used her best dishes on Wednesday, only as a reminder of when her mother died since the floral gold-rimmed dishes had been her mother's favorite.

"Pardon me, Lady Brinley."

She moved her gaze toward the door. Levi Montgomery stood just inside the room, looking solemn in his stance. She wanted to be mad at him, but it was difficult. Her mother always said that for a content life, one must not be quick to judge, but forgive easily.

"What do you need, Mr. Montgomery?"

He expelled a breath and stepped closer. "I need you not to hate me."

Inwardly, she groaned, recalling the way she had spoken to him earlier. "I'm sorry, Mr. Montgomery. I have had a trying morning, especially when my mother's precious dishes are in pieces."

Gretta's Gamble

"It was entirely my fault, for which I feel just awful about. I truly didn't mean for that to happen."

She dropped her gaze to her hands as she smoothed out the lap of her day dress. With his forlorn expression bearing deep into her soul, she feared that looking directly at him would be her undoing. He was entirely too handsome and charming for his own good. And, for hers.

"I appreciate your apology, and I forgive you." She peeked at him again. His expression had brightened with a hint of a smile. Her heart fluttered, so she lowered her gaze again.

"My lady, your forgiveness means the world to me." He moved closer to the sofa.

Inhaling a fortifying breath, she squared her shoulders and looked at him fully. "I suppose I should commend you for considering me more important than the dishes when I nearly fell down the stairs."

Levi shrugged. "When I realized you could get hurt, I didn't think twice. So, yes. You were more important. The dishes can be replaced. Your sweet presence cannot."

The way her heartbeat tripped over itself reminded her what an accomplished flirt he was, saying the right words to make a woman swoon. However, she would not be taken in by his charm. At least she hoped she was strong enough to resist. "I thank you, Mr. Montgomery."

He stepped closer. "Please, tell me what I can do to compensate for the loss of your favorite dishes."

"There isn't anything you can do." She folded her hands on her lap. "The tea service belonged to my mother, and she passed away not long after I married Lord Brinley."

Levi stopped at the edge of the sofa and knelt on one knee. She held her breath, wondering what he would do next since it was clear that he always surprised her one way or another.

"Lady Brinley, I promise you this now. I will do everything in my power to find a tea service that matches the one I broke."

Once again, her heartbeat skipped erratically, and she found her breathing uneven. This happened whenever he was near.

Just like what happened before when she felt like this, she couldn't tear her gaze away from his amazing blue eyes.

"No, Levi." She touched his arm. "That is not necessary. Please, don't worry yourself so much. I will soon put it from my mind."

His expression relaxed, and his smile widened. "You called me by my first name. I like the way it sounds coming from your mouth."

Oh, dear! Indeed, this conversation had taken a turn for the worse, and she must put an end to it now. After all, he was her servant, and she couldn't think of him any other way.

Gretta's Gamble

CHAPTER FIVE

Levi tried controlling his excitement. When he first came to talk to her, he doubted his charm would work. Now, seeing it in her eyes and hearing how her voice practically floated when she talked to him, he realized things were falling into place. If only his body wouldn't grow warm when she touched him, he might be able to think straight.

Although he still loved to charm women, he was determined to keep his vow in the wager he made with his friends. Levi would *not* allow a woman to control his heart ever again.

"Forgive me, Mr. Montgomery." She yanked her hand away. "That was a slip of the tongue. I shouldn't have—"

"It's fine, Lady Brinley. I don't mind at all if you call me Levi."

"But it's just not done. You are my servant, and I shouldn't be so personal with your name."

"What if I want us to be friends? I can assure you that friends call each other by their first names."

"Yes, but—"

"Then please, call me Levi when we are alone. You can keep protocol in front of the others, but I would like it very much if you would call me Levi."

She twisted her hands in her lap, and he wanted to touch her so she wouldn't feel so nervous. However, that might be pushing things at this point in their friendship.

"Please stand, Mr. Montgomery. The way you're kneeling in front of me, one might assume you are proposing."

"As you wish." He rose to his feet, continuing to watch her carefully. "Would you like me to do anything for you?"

"What do you mean?" she said in a rush as color climbed to her cheeks again.

Levi bit the inside of his cheek, hoping his face didn't look like he wanted to laugh. He didn't know why he made her nervous, but it felt nice knowing that he had some type of control over her as her *servant*.

"Conrad mentioned that you refused to take more tea after I had broken the service. I could fetch you some, if you would like."

Her shoulders fell as though she had exhaled deeply. "No, I'm fine. However, have you checked on my uncle yet?"

Blast it all. Obviously, she wanted him away from the room, but he didn't want to leave. They needed to discuss her brother, and he didn't know why she kept putting him off. But arguing with her at this point would be pointless.

"I haven't. Conrad has kept me busy. But I shall do so now."

"Thank you, Mr. Montgomery. Please, let me know how my uncle is faring today."

"I shall."

Levi gave her a nod before leaving the room. He gritted his teeth along the way. He understood why Gretta had wanted him to watch over her uncle, which had ultimately gotten him a position inside the manor, but he wanted to spend more time with her. He had to get her to trust him. He felt she might know where her brother was, even though she didn't realize she would have this information. Not only that, but she might have something that her brother stole, which Levi could use as evidence. But the longer he stayed as her servant, the farther Charles would run and even disappear for good.

Suddenly, he stopped. He didn't know where the old man's room was located, and that meant... He grinned. The countess needed to show him.

Levi's heartbeat picked up rhythm, and he swung around. She must have read his thoughts because she headed in his direction. He couldn't keep from admiring the way she looked today.

Gretta's Gamble

The creamy peach color of her gown complimented her complexion as well as her dark hair that hung in ringlets on her shoulders. Tempted, he wanted to touch her hair to see if it was as silky as it appeared.

"Mr. Montgomery?" She stopped a few steps away. "Do you know where my uncle's bedchamber is?"

Levi chuckled. "That was why I had stopped. I don't know where I'm going."

"Follow me. I'll show you."

Gretta moved down the hallway and he followed close behind. He shouldn't walk so near to her, and although she kept stepping away, he made certain that she wasn't too far. As they almost reached the end of the hallway, he purposely brushed his hand against hers. Her quick intake of air made him giddy.

Giddy? He must be addled. Men didn't feel giddy.

Gretta hurried ahead of him. He decided to let her this time. Perhaps he had disturbed her enough for one day—or at least for one afternoon.

She stopped at the door and knocked. "Uncle Reginald?" Slowly, she opened the door and peeked inside.

Levi held his breath, hoping she didn't find her uncle dead. For being so ill, Levi feared that would happen one of these days, and he didn't want her to be the first to see the old man in that condition. It would be devastating, to be sure.

Her shoulders relaxed, and a whoosh of air escaped her mouth. Levi sighed in relief. At least this wasn't the day God picked to take the older man.

"Uncle Reginald?" She opened the door wider and stepped inside. "I hope you are up for visitors."

"Visitors?" The old man rasped. "I would love some company."

As they neared the man's bedside, Gretta motioned with her hand toward Levi. "Do you remember Mr. Montgomery? He saved your life yesterday."

The man's happy expression quickly turned sour. "The man from prison?"

Levi groaned in silence. Apparently, that had been the wrong first impression to give a dying man. Perhaps he shouldn't have listened to Felix who had made the suggestion of playing a prisoner as a way to gain the countess's trust.

"Uncle Reginald," Gretta gasped. "You must not think of him that way. His only crime was to gamble when he didn't have the funds."

"And if you recall," the older man grumbled, "your husband did the same. It's a terrible vice and should not be tolerated." He lifted his chin haughtily. "What is he doing in my bedchambers? Has he come to add more bruises to my chest?"

Gretta lifted her chin stubbornly. "No, Uncle. Mr. Montgomery is my footman."

"*Footman?* Have you lost your mind?" The man gasped for air.

Gretta rushed up beside him and handed him the glass of water on the bedstand. "You must calm yourself, Uncle."

As the older man sipped his water, his glare met Levi's from over the rim of the glass. He had no idea how to help Gretta's uncle who was clearly against conversing with former prisoners. If he explained that he was really a Pinkerton agent, perhaps Lord Reynolds would feel differently. But that was a secret Levi couldn't share at this time.

Gretta set the glass back on the bedstand, straightened, and folded her arms. "Uncle Reginald, you must not get upset over trivial things. I'm in charge of your care, and I certainly know what is best for you." She motioned with her head toward Levi. "And I have put Mr. Montgomery in charge of caring for you, so I suggest you change your attitude very quickly."

Levi loved her firm voice, almost like a mother talking to a child. But the older man was so much like a needy child. Levi also couldn't believe how proud he felt at this moment that she would stick up for him in front of her uncle. Not many people would defend him as she had just done.

It was rather nice. And comforting.

Lord Reynolds calmed down as Levi and Gretta chatted with him, and after an hour, the old man didn't glare when he

Gretta's Gamble

looked at Levi. Thankfully, the lord became weary, and his eyes closed several times.

Having worked as a Pinkerton agent for several years, Levi had seen enough dead men to last a lifetime. Just before these men passed, the hue of their skin was a sickly gray, and dark circles made their eyes appear hollow. Poor Lord Reynolds certainly had one foot in the grave. Although Levi wasn't a physician, he didn't believe the older man would be with them much longer.

The countess moved from her chair and stepped closer to her uncle's bed. Levi quickly stood and watched her lean over and kiss the older man's cheek.

Levi wished he knew why his heart leapt as he watched the woman's lips briefly sweep her uncle's skin. She was so graceful, and so adorable. And for the life of him, he wondered why he imagined her doing that to him, but on his mouth, instead.

Mentally, he shook away the indecent thought. Things like that should never happen, especially since he was beginning to like the woman. Of course, once she discovered Levi's true purpose of being in her life, she would squash his feelings with the heel of her shoe.

He had no right to feel this way about her. No right at all.

As they left the man's bedchambers, Conrad stood in the hallway waiting. Levi groaned. The butler was going to yell at him again for not doing his duty, and of course, Levi didn't want to snap back at the man in front of their employer.

When Gretta noticed Conrad, she stopped. "Do you need something?"

"Actually, my lady, I was waiting for Mr. Montgomery. He was late meeting me in the dining room to start preparing for the evening meal."

She glanced at Levi and returned her attention to the butler. "Didn't you know he was with me?"

"I did, my lady."

"Well, he is doing what I asked him to do, which was care for my uncle. Is that not part of being a footman? After all, he did as I requested."

"Yes, of course. However, I need to still teach him—"

"Conrad," Levi interrupted. "I'm ready now. Shall we go to the dining room?"

The butler's face tightened. "Indeed, Mr. Montgomery."

Levi ran his gaze over Gretta's beautiful face again. He had thoroughly enjoyed the brief time they spent together, and he didn't want it to end. After all, they still hadn't talked about how to find her brother. If he did nothing else the rest of the evening, he would figure out a way to broach the subject and put a fire under her so that she would help him.

"Lady Brinley, I promise to check on your uncle later this evening when I'm finished in the dining room."

The stern expression she had when talking to the butler vanished and she gave Levi a smile. "I thank you, Mr. Montgomery."

As Levi followed the butler down the hall, he received the instinct impression that she was watching him. It was as if he *felt* her gaze moving over the back of him. Just before disappearing from her sight, he glanced over his shoulder. She hadn't moved, and just as he suspected, she was watching him.

He bit back a grin, shifting his focus to the dining room doors. Perhaps he needed to break this spell between them and meet her someplace private tonight. He would tell her it was to discuss her brother, but really, it would be to see if she was susceptible to a kiss.

There was no harm in sharing a kiss, especially when he knew nothing would come out of it. As she had mentioned before—he was her servant, and he certainly was *not* looking for a lasting relationship.

However, his heart accelerated in hopes that there would be more than just a simple kiss.

* * * *

Gretta's Gamble

Gretta paced the floor of her bedchambers, wringing her hands against her stomach. The evening meal had been terrible.

Mrs. Patterson cooked very tasty courses, and her uncle was able to attend and sit through the whole meal without falling asleep. The table had been set remarkably well for a man just learning his footman duties, and everything was immaculate. Under normal circumstances, that would mean the evening was a success.

But it wasn't. She blamed Levi Montgomery for being entirely too handsome and charming. And when he served the food with help from the kitchen maids, she was surprised to see him so well behaved. Not only that, but his evening attire made him appear more distinguished. Yet why couldn't she get the image out of her head when she saw him in the stable, brushing down the horse? If she was to pick which one she liked best, she would go with his casual appearance while in the stable.

Perhaps she should have left him with the horses where he was out of sight most of the day. With him outdoors, she may not have received a note from him that was left in her bedchamber.

It unnerved her that he had snuck into her room, but at the same time, butterflies danced in her stomach to think he had done something so daring.

She stopped at her vanity table and picked up the piece of paper, glancing over the writing once again.

Meet me in the stables tonight at eleven o'clock. We need to discuss how to find your brother. Levi.

It wasn't as if she had stopped thinking about finding her brother, but it seemed that with Levi always in her thoughts, her focus had become a little distracted. *Little?* She was lying to herself if she thought the handsome man's presence was *little* at all. He was a complete disruption in her life.

Indeed, it was time to focus more on her brother. However, meeting Levi in private was just not done. Once again, she must remind herself that he was a servant, and if she should meet him at all, other servants should be present.

Yet the temptation was too great. She wanted to know why he thought her brother was in danger. She wanted to know why they needed to help each other to find her brother. But most of all, she wanted to know why her body tingled whenever Levi was nearby. What was it about him that made it difficult to breathe whenever he touched her?

Until she could figure out what was wrong with her emotions, if she met him tonight in the stable, she would have to stay at least six feet away. Going against that rule could bring trouble and complications into her life. She certainly didn't need that.

The grandfather clock in the corridor chimed the eleventh hour. She groaned and rubbed her forehead. She would be foolish to meet Levi tonight. It would be foolish *not* to, as well.

How she loathed these types of decisions. But finding her brother was important to her.

Gretta spun around and grabbed her cloak. As she left her room, she whipped the garment around her shoulders and headed down the stairs. She took great care not to make any noise, even though she suspected the servants were asleep. But if they weren't, she didn't want to explain herself.

A gentle breeze swept through the trees as she headed toward the stable. The full moon guided her steps. She tried not to seem overeager, but she still found herself hurrying. Of course, she tried to convince herself that the reason she rushed was because she didn't want her servants seeing her night tryst.

As she entered the stable, she noticed only one lamp, but the amount of light it produced wasn't very much. Dare she ask what Levi's purpose for tonight's meeting was really about? Did he intend to seduce her? Although the idea was slightly flattering, she would let him know that his charm would not weaken her.

"Levi?" she asked softly, scanning her gaze around the stable.

"You are here."

Gretta's Gamble

His voice was so near it startled her, making her gasp and swing around. Why hadn't she seen him standing by the door? And why had he changed his clothes into the ones he wore when she first saw him in the stable that first day? *Oh, heavens...* This wasn't good at all.

"I..." She swallowed hard, trying to moisten her suddenly dry throat. "I didn't know if I would come or not."

"I'm very happy you came."

He stepped closer, so she took a step backward.

"I only came to talk about my brother," she said nervously.

"I know."

He moved closer, so she took two steps back.

"Mr. Montgomery, I believe we should keep our distance while discussing my brother."

He arched an eyebrow and gave her a silly grin. "I wish you would call me Levi."

Her heartbeat quickened. He was too handsome, and there were so many shadows. "Nevertheless, we should not stand too close."

"Why?"

Oh, for the nerve of that man. "You know perfectly well. I should not have to explain myself."

"Gretta, do I make you uncomfortable?"

Her heart fluttered. She shouldn't enjoy hearing him say her name so deeply. "This whole situation makes me nervous."

"Because we are alone?" He stepped closer.

She held up her hand to stop him. "I mean it, Levi. If you cannot keep your distance, I will return to the manor."

He sighed and folded his arms. "Then I'll stay right here."

She moved to one of the stalls and leaned against the gate. "I would very much like to discuss my brother and how we can help each other. After all, that is why I paid for your release from prison."

"Indeed, it was, and I'm relieved that you have realized that. All day long I wondered when you were going to say something about that."

"I couldn't very well have you as my footman without having you learn your duties, now could I? I had you running around, mainly as not to have my other servants suspicious of your actions."

He nodded slowly, but his crooked grin told her that he wasn't convinced.

"Now," she continued, "will you tell me why you think my brother is in danger?"

Levi slowly moved toward the same stall and stood across from her. Thankfully, he wasn't trying to get much closer like before. She truly didn't want to return to the manor so soon.

"There are things you don't know about Charles, and although I shouldn't say anything, I believe it might be the only way to find him."

A knot of dread lodged in her throat. Did she want to know about her brother's secret life? She knew he kept things from her because sisters tend to worry, but now she would learn what she had suspected all along.

Her brother was a thief.

Gretta's Gamble

CHAPTER SIX

Levi watched the countess cautiously, reading her expressions as they changed from anxiousness, to determination, and now, worry. When he finally found Charles Ramsay, he would wring that man's neck for adding this much unnecessary stress to his sister's life. She deserved none of the turmoil Charles put her through.

Levi adjusted his stance against the horse's stall wall, not because he was uncomfortable, but this was the only way to move closer to her in the slightest way possible. He must do it subtly so she wouldn't notice.

"What do you know about my brother?" she asked in a faint voice.

His chest tightened. Her distress was obvious. Although he didn't want to add more, he needed her to trust him. Having that connection with her was the only way to achieve his end goal.

"Are you certain you are ready to hear what I have to say?" Cautiously, he reached out and touched her arm resting along the top of the wooden plank. He waited for her to pull away, but she didn't.

Gretta nodded. "If it means to understand my brother better in order for us to find where he is hiding, then I must know everything."

"Do you recall when I told you I met your brother at the gaming tables?"

"I do."

"Charles and I spent time in places like that, and on a few occasions, I realized he was..." He paused, hoping that the news wouldn't overly upset her.

"He was what?" she urged.

"Cheating."

She gasped and her body stiffened. "Cheating?"

Levi nodded. "I have a talent for noticing things like that, whereas other men may not. However, with your brother, he wasn't very good at covering his flaw. In fact, I can recall three instances where the men he was cheating called him on it before dragging him out of the building to... um... knock some sense into him."

He wasn't certain how to phrase it to a woman's sensibilities, and he prayed she would understand the meaning. By the whiteness of her fingers because of her clenched fists, he realized she knew what he was hinting at.

"Gretta," he said, gently stroking her arm. "I know that you see him as your innocent brother, but I assure you, he knows how to take care of himself. He knows how to fight back."

Gradually, her body relaxed. "He wasn't hurt too terribly bad during these times the other men knocked some sense into him?"

"He wasn't. I promise."

She shook her head. "And yet, my foolish brother continued to cheat at cards?"

"He did, and soon he became better at it."

"Do you cheat as well?"

Levi wanted to laugh at her assumption but dared not make a mockery of her pain. "No. Although I have the ability to notice others do it, I have never felt compelled to be dishonest like that."

He had to be careful with what he said so as not to make the lie any bigger than it already was. The truth was very close to his story. He had watched Charles in action at the gaming tables, and even witnessed the man being dragged out back of the building in a series of fisticuffs. The only thing Levi lied about was being friends with her brother.

Gretta's Gamble

It was quite nice to be able to tell the truth once in a while. In fact, knowing he wasn't lying soothed his soul. He wished he could do it more often, but his job required him to be dishonest with people so that he could obtain information.

She sighed and relaxed her hands. "Do you believe my brother was taken by one of the men he cheated?"

"No. Your brother was clever with his words and could seduce a nun if he had to." She blushed and he tried not to chuckle. "However, I think that your brother is on the run from men who are after him because of what he has done."

Her eyes watered. "My brother is a thief, isn't he?"

Levi hesitated to answer. Did she know about the necklace her brother had stolen from the wealthy widow? Giving away his purpose wasn't what Levi wanted to do at this moment. "What do you mean?"

"He takes money from men dishonestly, and to me, that makes him a thief."

Levi exhaled slowly. "I suppose you could put it in those terms."

She stepped toward him. "If Charles were to get caught, would he be arrested and thrown into prison?"

"Yes, I'm sure of it, mainly because he makes a living doing things like that."

A frown marred her pretty face, and the liquid in her eyes doubled. A pain ripped through his chest as if someone had twisted a knife inside him. He couldn't handle seeing her in this state, and once again, he cursed Charles for making his sister suffer so much.

Gretta's breaths were unsteady. "I don't wish to see my brother in prison, but if it will help him change his ways, then so be it."

"You are a wise woman." Levi slid his touch to her cold fingers and gently rubbed to bring warmth back into her body. "Charles should consider himself very fortunate to have a sister with such a kind heart who wants to look after him."

The corners of her perfectly shaped mouth lifted, resembling a smile.

"And my brother is very fortunate to have such a caring friend who will do anything to bring him to justice."

His heart melted, yet at the same time, regret for deceiving the countess grew inside him like a festering disease. Indeed, justice needed to be served. Charles Ramsay would pay for what he had done.

"Levi?" her voice trembled.

He enjoyed the way she spoke his name. If only she would permit him to tell her this, but since he was just a servant, she wouldn't allow it. "Yes?"

"Do you think my brother is... dead?"

A tear slid down her cheek, and he couldn't handle seeing her in this much pain. She may push him away, but he wanted to comfort her the only way he knew how.

"Oh, Gretta." He closed the space between them and took her in his arms where she came willingly, resting her head against his chest. "You mustn't think such things. You mustn't give up hope."

"How can I not after all my brother has done?"

Her voice broke in sorrow, and Levi pulled her closer, caressing her back. He had never been able to watch while a woman broke down emotionally, and this particular woman was slowly sneaking into his heart, which meant he had to try harder to stop it from happening.

"Your brother is a fighter. I have seen how he takes care of himself. I don't believe he is dead."

"However will we find him?"

"I think one of your servants might know."

She arched an eyebrow in question. "Why do you think that?"

"If any of yours or Lord Brinley's servants knew Charles, they might know something. I'm hoping they will have information that would lead us in the right direction."

She clutched his shirt and tilted her head back to peer into his eyes. "I don't care who you ask, but we need to find him, Levi. Uncle Reginald will die soon, and I shall never forgive myself if I cannot bring Charles back home to say his last goodbyes."

Levi groaned under his breath. If he wasn't feeling guilty enough for deceiving her, now he felt even worse for wanting to arrest the thief. But she was correct. Charles Ramsay needed to see his uncle one last time.

If only they could find Gretta's brother in time.

* * * *

Gretta knew what she was doing. She was in Levi's arms of her own accord. At the moment it didn't matter that he was a servant. All she cared about was being comforted by this incredibly strong man with a kind heart and gentle touch.

She pressed her face against his muscular chest, trying to fight the sobs threatening to pour out of her at any moment. She needed this more than she needed food. Loneliness had been her constant companion for too long—even when she was married. Now that she had someone to share this moment with, she would not pass it up just because he was a servant and she, a noblewoman.

"Yes, my sweet Gretta," he whispered tightly. "Your brother should see his uncle before he dies."

It broke her heart to realize Charles wasn't the man she had idolized. They had been close as siblings, but after her marriage to Frederick, she and Charles drifted apart. If ever she needed a big brother, it was during the time of not having friends as the countess.

She inhaled slowly, trying to get control of her tears. She hadn't wanted to cry in front of Levi. Crying made her weak. She wanted to be the strong woman she portrayed to society. She didn't want Levi to think any less of her.

Slowly, she tilted back her head to look up into his handsome face. He pulled back just enough to meet her stare. Shadows were everywhere, and although she could see the outline of his face, she could not see the color of his eyes. But she knew they were a brilliant blue.

As she skimmed her gaze over his face, she realized he had the most masculine features. His nose was perfectly straight, and not too wide. His cheekbones were high but placed evenly. And his mouth... She sighed. He had the most remarkable lips. When he frowned, she felt it all the way to her heart. And when he smiled, she melted.

"Gretta," he said huskily, cupping the side of her face. "You should not be staring at me like that."

"Like what?" A different rhythm took over her heartbeat, and she suddenly became breathless.

He smiled lazily. "You are looking at me as if you are enjoying yourself in my arms."

Could he really see that in her expression? She must not know how to hide her feelings very well.

"Don't you like how I'm looking at you?"

He chuckled deeply. "Oh, Gretta. That is the problem. I like it too much."

The pad of his thumb slid across her cheek, heading closer to her mouth. Her heartbeat quickened.

"The question should be," he continued. "Do *you* like looking at me as though I was a tasty morsel?"

If the mood hadn't turned so personal, she would have laughed out loud. But his calming voice mesmerized her, and his sultry gaze made her feel giddy. Perhaps she did like looking at him as if he was delicious food. Then again, *like* was not the correct word for the direction her thoughts were heading. She quite enjoyed studying his face this closely, feeling his warm breath against her skin.

"Levi, you are an extremely handsome man. Any woman would be a fool not to enjoy the view."

One side of his mouth lifted higher than the other. She nearly sighed with contentment knowing she was the one who made him act this way.

His chest shook in silent laughter, but soon he stepped back, releasing her. It was concerning to feel the cold emptiness consuming her body. She folded her arms, hoping to bring back some heat.

Gretta's Gamble

"Forgive me for not thinking of your welfare." Levi moved to retrieve his jacket hanging over one of the stall's doors. He brought it back to her and placed it over her shoulders. "I shouldn't keep you out here any longer. Go inside where it's warmer."

She should. After all, it was improper to be out here with him in the first place. But going inside meant that she would have to wait until morning to see him again. Sleep certainly wouldn't come easily after hearing about her brother, and especially since she would remember how it felt to be in Levi's arms, wondering if it would happen again.

"Yes, I should get back inside, but—"

"But what?"

"I suppose we should talk again. After all, I definitely need your help with finding my brother."

"Yes, Gretta. I think we should talk again. However, I'm sure Conrad will have me busy tomorrow, just as I was today. I'm sure he will become suspicious if he realizes we have had a lengthy conversation, since I know it's not generally done."

"Do you think we should meet in private again?" Her heartbeat increased, just imagining the possibilities.

"We might have to. I don't want to ruin your reputation."

"Indeed, and I don't want my servants thinking I'm giving you special attention."

"Then shall we meet here again tomorrow night to formulate a plan to find your brother?"

She nodded. "Yes."

His gaze dropped to her mouth, and she became breathless. He caressed her cheek, but then his thumb brushed across her bottom lip. *Oh, heavens!* She could scarcely catch her breath. Why was he making it so difficult to leave?

"Do you want me to walk you back to the manor?"

Slowly, she shook her head, not able to remove her gaze from his handsome face. "I shall be fine."

As she remained in place, the seconds passed by, and although she should move, her feet were rooted to the ground. If she continued in this trance, he might think she wanted him to kiss her, no matter how improper the idea was. But oh, she was certain this man knew how to kiss to make her swoon, and the longer she stared at him, the more she was sure he would try to steal a kiss. But would she willingly return the affection?

She swallowed hard once more, not only moistening her dry throat, but trying to gain the courage to pull away. But she must. She couldn't let this man steal her heart. After all, he wasn't husband material at all, especially if he was friends with her brother.

Finding the courage, she pulled away from him and removed his jacket from across her shoulders. "I thank you for your assistance. Have a good rest, and I'll talk to you tomorrow."

As he took the jacket, his grin widened. "I fear sleep isn't going to come easily since all I'll think about is meeting you again in private."

On shaky legs, Gretta walked out of the stable and toward the manor. She was sure her dreams would be pleasant tonight, but come morning, she must remember he was her servant, and he was only working for her to pay back his debt. And no matter what, she couldn't let him touch her again.

Gretta's Gamble

CHAPTER SEVEN

Actually, Levi had a wonderful night's sleep, but he was very eager to wake up before dawn to get himself ready for the day. It still irritated him that he had to continue with his role as Gretta's footman, but he had been in worse situations while undercover as an agent, but for some reason, this was the assignment that bothered him the most. In all of the other cases, he was able to control how fast—or slow—he would progress in the investigation. Yet he couldn't do that with Gretta. Her servants would certainly become suspicious if he acted like he was controlling everything.

And speaking of Gretta's servants... It was time he started asking questions. One of the servants who had been with Gretta for all this time must know something about Charles Ramsay's disappearance. Levi's gut feeling told him so.

"Mr. Montgomery," Conrad snapped. "Would you please pay attention?"

Levi wished he could completely ignore the butler, but since the man was supposed to be over the footman, Levi had no other choice.

"Pardon me," Levi apologized with a clenched jaw. "I fear I have much on my mind."

"Well, you are at work now, and your mind should be occupied with your duties."

Levi nodded. "I understand. So, what is it that you need me to do today?"

Conrad lifted his chin haughtily. "You will be helping the maids clean the manor. You will move the furniture so they can sweep and mop the floors, then you will put the furniture back exactly how it was. After that, you can carry firewood and coal to the bedchambers and stock that for the night. Once you have that completed, you will help the kitchen maids prepare the afternoon meal."

Levi bunched his hands into fists by his sides as he listened to the instructions. With everything the butler wanted him to do, when was Levi going to see Gretta? The only good thing about his morning duties was that he would be able to question some of the servants. Hopefully, one of them would help in searching for Charles.

"Fine," he told the butler. "Just let me know what room the maids plan on cleaning first, and I'll move the furniture."

Conrad pointed toward the end of the corridor. "They always start on the south side of the manor and work their way to the other side. I just talked to Mrs. Franklin, and she informed me that the maids are collecting their cleaning supplies as we speak."

"Then that will give me a few minutes to check on Lord Reynolds."

Conrad's face tightened. "I don't think—"

"One of my duties," Levi quickly interrupted the butler, "is caring for Lord Reynolds. Lady Brinley specifically assigned that to me, and I *will* do whatever she asks."

Conrad pulled out his timepiece from his pocket. "You have exactly ten minutes, and not a second later."

Levi rolled his eyes. This particular servant was going to drive him insane, he was certain of it.

He quickly turned away from the butler and hurried toward Lord Reynold's room. Although he thought Gretta was probably still in bed asleep, he hoped to see her sometime this morning, but he seriously doubted she was already with her uncle.

Levi reached the door and quietly opened it. The drapes were pulled closed, and the only light was a small lamp near his bed, and the glowing embers from the fireplace.

He took soft steps to the hearth first, adding a couple of logs, and with the poker, moved the embers until the wood caught on fire. Then he quietly moved toward Lord Reynold's bed.

It was still difficult to tell if the man was alive or dead, only because of the pallor of his skin. Sadly, the man didn't have many more days before he passed on. Levi only hoped the old man would hang on until after they found Charles since it was Gretta's wish that her brother say his last goodbyes to their uncle.

Levi stood by his bed, watching closely to see if the man was breathing. Studying Lord Reynold's nightshirt, Levi concentrated on seeing any movement. After a few seconds passed without seeing him breathing, panic filled Levi and he stepped closer.

He placed his fingers under the old man's nose but didn't feel anything. Levi quickly laid his fingers along the man's neck, hoping to feel a pulse. Finally, he felt it, but it was weak.

"Lord Reynolds?" Levi asked as he gently touched his shoulder and shook him. "Will you open your eyes and look at me?"

The man didn't budge.

Levi leaned closer and shook him harder, but not too much because the man bruised easily. "Lord Reynolds, you cannot go yet. Wait until we find Charles."

Still, there was no response.

"Lord Reynolds," Levi said louder. "You cannot leave Gretta. It will break her heart, and you don't want to do that."

Finally, the man moved his head just as a low groan released from his throat. Levi sighed in relief.

Lord Reynold's eyelids blinked open, and he stared dumbfounded at Levi. "Pray, what are you blabbering about?"

Levi wanted to chuckle but resisted. "Forgive me for startling you, but I was just checking to see how you were doing this morning."

The man scowled and glanced toward the window. When he met Levi's stare again, his scowl darkened. "Are you addled? It's not morning yet."

"Forgive me, Lord Reynolds, but the sun is indeed up, and since your niece assigned me to look after you, I needed to do that before Conrad put me to work doing other things."

"Fine, you have checked on me." Reynolds flipped his hand. "Now leave so I can get more sleep."

"As you wish."

Levi headed for the door, but just before reaching it, Gretta walked inside. Surprised, he hitched a breath, and then when he beheld her beauty, he sighed heavily. She was certainly a vision this morning, wearing a cream-colored day dress with bell-shaped sleeves and a square-neck bodice. The light material made her brown hair appear even darker, which she wore long and flowing over her shoulders with the sides pulled back with hair combs. Her lips also appeared like raspberries, full and ready to devour.

Now he was the one fighting to breathe normally. He had never met a woman who made him this breathless.

She gasped lightly. "Good morning, Levi."

"Good morning, Gretta."

"I'm happy to see you are already checking on my uncle." She glanced toward the bed and then quickly returned her attention to him. "How is he doing?"

"Your uncle is fine." Levi kept his voice low as not to disturb the old man. "Of course, he is a little irritable this morning since I woke him up."

Grinning, she stepped closer to Levi and touched his arm. "To be quite honest, Uncle Reginald is irritable most days."

Levi smiled, loving that she felt so comfortable touching him. "But I must say, I'm happier about seeing you this early in the morning. I thought you would still be asleep."

Her cheeks grew pink, and she removed her hand from his arm. "I didn't think I would see you so soon, either. But I'm an early riser, mainly so that I can check on my uncle."

"Then I'm glad we got to see each other." He winked. "Even if it was in this room."

She glanced at the hearth, then to the window, before stopping on her uncle. "I thank you for checking on him." Her eyes moved back to meet with Levi's. "It pleases me that you are doing as I have asked."

He cocked his head. "Why wouldn't I? After all, I'm your footman, and..." He stepped closer and caressed her cheek. "And hopefully, you can trust me enough to be your friend."

"Yes. We are friends."

He sighed in satisfaction. At least that goal had been accomplished. Now, to get the other ones done, as well. "Unfortunately, I am needed in the south end of the manor. Conrad is having me move furniture for the maids."

She smiled and stepped away. "Then I shan't keep you another moment."

"I hope we see each other again soon. I don't know if I can wait until tonight when we meet in the stable before talking to you again."

She chuckled lightly. "I'm sure I'll see you before then."

"Splendid. I look forward to it."

He moved to the door but glanced over his shoulder at her before leaving. To his delight, she had been watching him. As he walked out of the room grinning widely, he wished her presence didn't excite him so much.

The next few hours practically crept by. It became tedious to move the furniture, and then to wait for the maids to sweep and mop before he could move everything back. The maids appeared to be around Gretta's age, perhaps slightly older, but not much. Christine was the prettier of the two, and the one who giggled the most whenever he said something to her. After a while, her insistent stares and batting her eyes at him began to wear on his already frazzled nerves. Still, he didn't want to do anything to upset the servants. Not if he still sought information from them.

When the women stopped chattering, he knew it was his turn to start a conversation. He cleared his throat, getting their attention, and then gave them his practiced charming smile.

"I hope you don't mind me asking, but how long have you worked for Lady Brinley?"

Christine stopped and rested against the mop. Her eyes twinkled when she looked at him.

"I have been with the countess since she and her husband first set up residency in New York." She nodded toward the other maid who appeared slightly older. "And Beth was with Lady Brinley while they were still in England."

Now he realized it was Beth he needed to charm since she must have known Charles more than Christine.

"I wish I could have known Lord Brinley," Levi said. "I'm sure he was a good man."

Beth nodded. "One of the best, Mr. Montgomery."

"Did you know Lady Brinley before she became a countess?" he wondered.

"No. I was hired by Lord Brinley right after they were wed."

"Well, I'm glad Lady Brinley has such devoted servants. She needs you more now than before."

Christine arched an eyebrow. "Why do you say that?"

"Well, because her brother is missing, and her uncle is…" He didn't dare say *dying*, even though the man was certainly at death's door. "Her uncle is unwell, so she will need trusted servants by her side to help her stay strong."

Christine frowned. "Indeed, she does."

"That was just so upsetting what happened with her brother," he added, then frowned to show his sympathy for Gretta's misery.

"Do you mean about him disappearing the way he did?" Beth asked.

Levi nodded. "Yes. From what I heard, her brother wouldn't have just left on his own without letting his sister know."

Beth nodded. "They were certainly close, but I must say, I wasn't impressed with the man."

Levi was grateful she had given him an opening to keep prying into the man's life. "Why is that?"

"He was a selfish man, and acted as though he didn't care at all about his sister's welfare."

Gretta's Gamble

That surprised Levi, especially since most older brothers cared about their younger siblings and wanted to protect them. "How did the countess feel about that?"

"Well, I realize you are new here, and that you don't know her well, but Lady Brinley has the kindest heart. I'm sure it hurt her that Charles didn't care about her much, but Lady Brinley wasn't about to show it."

"I met him before I became Lady Brinley's servant," Christine interjected. "All he wanted was to take advantage of me and I wasn't about to let him. And if you ask me, I'm sure he stepped over the line with some woman and maybe he was forced to wed. That would explain his disappearance."

Levi wasn't shocked to hear that Charles Ramsay was both a thief and a rogue, but it upset him that the man didn't care one iota about his younger sister. Beth was correct in assuming that Levi didn't know Gretta well, but the woman did have a caring heart. Not every woman would pay a stranger's debt to get out of prison, even though she didn't know Levi and his friend had staged it.

But what Christine said about being forced to wed, he didn't think a man like Charles would allow anyone to force him into doing *that*. However, Levi wouldn't doubt that some injured woman may have kidnapped him for revengeful purposes. In that case, the next place Levi needed to look for more information was in brothels.

"Then I'm glad the countess has the two of you on her side." Levi smiled once more, hoping to give them encouragement because Gretta needed more friends.

Beth snapped her fingers, gaining Christine's attention as she pointed to the floor. "We best make haste and get our cleaning done. If not, both Mrs. Franklin and Conrad will be down on us for slacking in our duties."

Levi let the maids continue to clean, and he moved the furniture in each room as they moved along. Finally, it was time to carry the coal and firewood. Christine carried the bucket of coal, while Levi loaded his arms with the wood. Thankfully, there were only a few main rooms that needed these items.

From what he had overheard from the maids, Gretta only used the parlor, the sitting room, and the dining area besides her own bedchamber. It was up to the servants to refill their own rooms with coal and wood.

Gretta's bedchamber was the last, and as he entered in the daylight, he scanned everywhere, getting to know the layout. When he left her the missive last night about meeting him in the stable, it had been dark, and shadows were everywhere. There had been no time to snoop then, but now... He wished Christine would leave so that he could look through Gretta's jewelry. If he found Mrs. Kensington's heart-shaped ruby necklace, he would certainly ask Gretta how she came to obtain it, and he would confess to his true profession and that he wanted to arrest her brother.

Christine hummed a tune as she scooped out the ashes from the hearth into an empty bucket. Levi restacked the wood, making it accessible for Gretta to get to if needed during the night. Every so often, he glanced at her vanity and at the jewelry box that sat in the corner. At least he now knew where to look in the dark when he came back to the room sometime after hours.

He also kept moving his gaze to the bed. Images filled his head of what Gretta would look like in her nightdress with her hair straight and hanging over her shoulders as she prepared for sleep. He wished he could stop the dreams filling his head of her pressed up against him while in his arms, just as she had been last night at the stable, but he could still feel her imprint that had warmed him.

Shaking his head, he tried focusing on the task at hand. She obviously knew he had been in her room last night since she had gotten his note, but how much had she thought about him being in her bedchambers? Could this be the next place they met in private instead of the stable? He was sure she wouldn't agree to it.

He stood and brushed his palms against his thighs. Christine rose as well but didn't take the buckets. Confusion filled him, making him wonder if he should offer to take them since his arms weren't occupied with the wood any longer.

"Levi," she said huskily, moving closer and resting her hands on his chest.

He groaned in silence, knowing what she had in mind, which of course, she wouldn't get. "Christine, I don't think—"

"Please, don't try and stop me, Levi." Her gaze moved to his mouth. "I can feel the sparks between us, and I think we shouldn't fight this attraction."

"Christine, I'm flattered but—"

Before he could finish, she lifted up and pressed her mouth against him. This wasn't the first time he had come across a woman so bold, and just like the others, he knew how to stop things before the situation became worse.

He gripped her shoulders and pushed her back, ready to give her a lecture, but then a woman's gasp ricocheted through the room, and he swung his attention toward the door. Gretta stood with her hand on her throat, and with wide eyes, throwing him an accusing glare.

Levi silently swore. This was not what he wanted to happen. Just as he had gained Gretta's trust, now he lost it.

CHAPTER EIGHT

Gretta didn't know whether to be angry or hurt. But for appearance's sake, she must not show that what she witnessed hurt her in any way.

She straightened her shoulders and bunched her hands into fists, switching her focus between Levi and the maid, not knowing who to blame. Was it his fault that he was so charmingly handsome and made the woman's heart flutter? Or was the maid so free with her kisses that she would give herself to any man who smiled at her?

"Oh, Lady Brinley," Christine said in a rush. "Please, forgive us. It's not what it looks like."

Gretta rolled her eyes. "I don't care that you're kissing each other, but don't think I'm a simpleton, because it indeed looks exactly like what I think it is. However, this is *my* quarters, and *my* bedchamber. If you want to show your affection for each other, do not ever do it in my room again, or I will fire you both. Understood?"

"Lady Brinley," Levi said, stepping toward her. "Please, allow me to explain."

"Finish stocking the firewood and coal in my bedchamber, and then leave. I don't want to see either of you for the rest of the day."

Before they could say anymore, Gretta hurried out of the room. She had been ready to go riding and had wanted to find Levi first. When she heard he was stocking the rooms with firewood, she searched to find him. Now she wished she hadn't.

At least she was ready to ride, which was why it didn't take her long before hurrying down the stairs and out of the manor. The groomsman had her horse saddled and ready. As soon as the servant helped her mount, she took off. Behind her, she heard someone calling her name. Without looking, she knew who it was, but at this moment, she didn't want to see Levi, just as she had told him and Christine.

She rode her horse hard, but it didn't make the image of what she saw leave her head. The maid's eyes were glassy as if she had been drinking too many spirits, yet Gretta knew it was Levi's kiss that had made the woman look so elated. His hands had been on her shoulders, as if he held her up against his muscular body for the mere pleasure of being close to her.

Having been the recipient of Levi's heated stares and tender caresses, Gretta knew exactly what her maid had felt. It irritated her that she felt a stab of jealousy when she walked in on the servants' tender moment. Gretta knew better than to fall for the man's charm, yet she still allowed it to happen.

Perhaps if she hadn't been so lonely, she would have been able to resist him. If only she'd been happy in her marriage, she wouldn't have looked at Levi as God's answer to her prayers.

Thankfully, this had happened before she let Levi charm her more than he had already done. Now she knew what kind of man he really was, she wanted him out of her life. However, before she threw him out of her home, they needed to find her brother. Levi had been Charles' friend, and wanted to find him as much as she did.

When she reached a small stream, she stopped the horse and dismounted. She took the reins and led the animal to the water to drink.

Her life had been miserable from the day she married Frederick. During their courtship, he had made her feel like the most precious woman in England. He had given her trinkets and took her to balls, boasting to his friends about their engagement. But the minute he repeated the wedding vows, something in him changed, and he didn't want to spend time with her. He enjoyed going hunting with his friends instead of staying home with his bride.

She had made friends with her servants after that, knowing they would be the ones to keep her company during the day.

But then Frederick announced that he was tired of the *ton's* rules and wanted to live in America. He had been told of speculations he could invest in that would make him rich. Because she was his wife, she couldn't argue with him, even if she didn't want to leave her family. Then again, Charles had come to New York first, and in his letters, he mentioned how much better life was here than in England.

Gretta released a heavy sigh and leaned her forehead against the horse's neck. The sooner Charles was found, the quicker she could get Levi out of her life. And if she wanted to find a man to make her swoon, she certainly wouldn't look for him at the prison.

And what about Christine? That woman flaunted herself to any man who paid any attention. If the woman hadn't come with a good reference, Gretta would have dismissed her a while ago. She didn't have many friends, mainly because she stayed close to home caring for Uncle Reginald. Even though Christine irritated her at this moment, at least she was someone to talk to on occasion.

The vision of Christine and Levi in a lover's embrace turned her stomach. It was a scene she never wanted to see again. Gretta mounted her horse once more. Riding hard would get her mind far from her troubles. Just her and the open road. Freedom… yet loneliness.

Taking a deep breath and then releasing it slowly. This wasn't much different than Frederick staying out all night or gambling away their fortune. All she needed to do was hold her head high and move one. After all, she was a countess, and she had indeed earned the title for what she had to put up with while married.

She kicked her heels against the side of the horse and took off in another strong gallop. The wind brushed past her face as she held it high, hoping the coolness on her skin would wash away the pain of isolation. If she hadn't married Frederick, maybe her life would have been better. But thinking of the *what-ifs* from her past wasn't wise.

Gretta's Gamble

Everything happened for a reason. Being widowed at an early age could only mean one thing. There was still more she must experience, and she didn't think it was in America. After she found Charles, she would convince him to return with her to England where their real friends lived. There was nothing for her here, not anymore.

Her temples throbbed so she slowed the horse. Gretta put one of her hands up to the back of her neck and rubbed. She must return home and rest to get rid of this blasted headache. Sadly, her afternoon ride needed to be cut short. She just prayed she wouldn't have to see Levi or Christine before reaching her room to rest. It was bad enough they wouldn't leave her mind, but she didn't dare face them again today.

* * * *

There was no way to turn back the hands of time. Christine was out of line for making advances toward him, and he wanted to let Gretta know, but when he had rushed out after her, it was too late. She rode off on her horse without even looking back at him.

This wasn't supposed to happen this way. Maybe if he hadn't cleaned up after being released from prison, his offensive appearance would have appalled Christine. But then, it would have done the same to Gretta.

She had been gone for a while, and he doubted she had any intention of returning soon. From the look on her face, he knew she had been hurt by what she witnessed between him and Christine. Because he had been observing Gretta's routine, he knew that when she went riding, she was usually gone for an hour, and sometimes longer, which meant…

If he was going to snoop through her bedchamber for the necklace, now was the time to do it.

He was downstairs again, but none of the other servants were anywhere nearby. Cautiously, he glanced up and down the hallway, searching for Conrad. That man had the eyes of an eagle, and they were always on Levi. He didn't need the butler to stop his endeavors now.

Slowly, he made his way up the stairs, pausing briefly at every sound. When he made it to the top floor, he took soft steps toward her bedchamber. Once he reached the door, he paused, listening again for any signs that someone was nearby. Satisfied that he was alone, he entered.

Gretta's room was empty, just as he had hoped it would be. The drapes were opened over the large window, allowing sunlight to brighten the room.

He couldn't stop his gaze from moving to the large canopy bed. It was definitely the type of bed a countess would sleep in. Large fluffy pillows covered the head, and a pale-blue checkered quilt was folded nicely at the foot. This was much nicer than the thin mattress and worn ropes on the frame where he slept in the servants' quarters. He shouldn't feel jealous, after all, he was only playing the part she labeled him, which meant nice accessories did not come with it.

He moved quickly to her vanity. Levi flipped open the rectangle-shaped velvet jewelry box, and immediately a tune started playing. He shut it just as quickly. Listening carefully, to make sure no one heard the music, he tried it again, slowly, slipping his finger over the mechanism that triggered the tune.

Inside were many jewels, but immediately he noticed a sapphire necklace and matching earbobs. She had been wearing this yesterday because it made him want to caress her earlobe. He then noticed a sparkling wedding band nestled in its own velvet slot, but nowhere could he see Mrs. Kensington's heart-shaped ruby necklace.

He grumbled under his breath. Why wasn't it here? All of her other jewelry was in this location. Then again, perhaps Charles had given her the jewelry and told her to keep it in a safe place. The thief would have done that so as not to be caught with the stolen necklace.

Levi closed the jewelry box then rummaged through the drawer on the vanity. Hair pins of different colors were in there, along with her brush. He picked it up, and immediately, her honeysuckle scent wafted around him.

Closing his eyes, he smiled as butterflies grew inside his stomach. He really needed to talk with her and explain the scandalous scene she witnessed, and how he tried to push Christine away, which was when Gretta walked in. He didn't care about the maid, but he didn't know how to get that through Gretta's head. But as long as he could gain her trust again, that is what mattered.

He placed her brush back inside the drawer and closed it. Levi moved away from the vanity and headed toward the closet. Suddenly, the bedroom door pushed open, stopping him in his tracks. He whipped around just as Gretta noticed him. Her eyes widened and her mouth dropped open as though she was going to scream.

"Gretta, don't." He stepped toward her, holding up his hands in surrender. "It's just me, and I'm not going to hurt you."

She scowled. "Mr. Montgomery, why do I keep catching you in my bedchamber?"

"I—I was waiting for you. I need to speak with you about what happened earlier." His jumbled mind tried to find the right words to say.

"I thought I made it clear that I didn't want to see you or Christine for the rest of the day." She folded her arms.

"You made it very clear, but I couldn't let you continue to think the wrong thing. Nothing happened with me and the maid."

She arched an eyebrow. "Indeed? Then I suppose you were holding her still so that your lips could pluck some type of foreign object out of her mouth?"

He groaned in silence. Even though she mentioned earlier that she didn't care if he was kissing Christine, it was obvious that Gretta did care. Why else would she be so upset?

"Please, Gretta... Lady Brinley, will you let me explain? It breaks my heart that you had to see that, especially when it was all one-sided. I assure you, I did not want to kiss her. I wouldn't do anything like that and ruin our friendship. Please believe me."

Gretta stood in silence. He could tell she was contemplating her next move. Levi was taking a great risk since he knew she could throw him out, but he had to do something. Plus, he had to make her think he was in her room to talk, not to snoop through her things.

"Fine," she finally replied, straightening her shoulders. "But we cannot talk here. It's improper."

"Then walk with me in the garden, I beg you."

"Give me a few moments to change out of my riding outfit. I will meet you outside in thirty minutes."

He nodded. "That will give me enough time to slip downstairs and check on your uncle again." He hoped his caring words about her relative would soften her heart.

At least she agreed to talk. Now, he must think of the right words to convince her that he had no feelings for the maid. He didn't need her as an enemy right now, especially since he could feel himself growing attached to her, something he vowed would never happen again.

Levi hurried out of her room without being noticed. This would be the longest thirty minutes ever. He made every effort to go down a different corridor just to not be seen by Conrad. He wasn't sure what it was about that man, but Levi didn't like him. Perhaps it was the overprotective way Conrad hovered around Gretta as if she was a precious piece of glass. Or maybe it was the way the butler thought that everything in the manor should be in tip-top shape and in the exact spot it had been in before the cleaning. Personally, Levi didn't think rooms could get that dirty so quickly.

While checking on Uncle Reginald, Levi refreshed the man's tea, and added a few more logs to the fire. The old man continued to throw invisible daggers with his glare toward Levi, but he didn't blame the man. After all, Levi had come from prison.

Thankfully, the man didn't talk much, and so Levi was able to excuse himself and leave. He hurried to the closest side door, praying that Conrad wouldn't stop him. It was very important to talk to Gretta today. He couldn't have her thinking he was charming all her maids.

In fact, the only woman he wanted to charm was Gretta. One way or another, he would earn her trust.

CHAPTER NINE

Gretta inherited her love for flower gardens from her mother, and when Frederick moved them to New York, she was determined to have the nicest lawns in the city. If Gretta wasn't out riding, she was tending to her flowers. Thankfully, the late spring was showing blossoms on most of the flowers, but it seemed that nobody at the estate appreciated her garden as much as she... which was why it surprised her to see Levi moving around each different colored rose bush and bending to sniff each flower. Most men didn't take the time to appreciate the beauty of her garden.

He still wore his footman uniform, and she wished he didn't look so refined. Certainly, he was not made to wear these clothes. He was a snake, and she must remember that.

She had changed into a pale-green day dress. There was no time to coil her hair, so she brushed it away from her face and tied the bulk at the base of her neck with a matching ribbon. And this definitely wasn't the occasion to wear jewelry, either.

Exhaling a deep breath, she lifted her chin and walked toward him, holding in her dignity. She didn't want him to see how he had hurt her earlier, even though she feared he already knew.

He must have heard her coming, because he snapped upright and faced her. His smile was charming, yet sincere.

"I take it you are enjoying the scents?" she asked, pointing to the rose bushes.

He nodded. "They are so lovely just as they bloom, and you have so many."

"Yes, well... I was taught well. My mother also loved flower gardens."

He stepped toward her. "I must admit, I've never been in one. There are people I meet that have rose bushes, but not of every color and design."

She shrugged. "I enjoy their beauty."

"Forgive me for saying, but I fear once you are amongst the flowers, your beauty outshines them all."

She wanted to roll her eyes, especially since she had heard that line before from other men and didn't believe it then, either. However, the flutters in her belly reminded her how much she enjoyed his flirtation. She cursed her weakness. There must be a way to stay strong.

"Shall we move on to the next matter at hand?" She folded her arms. "You were going to explain to me why you and Christine were in my bedchamber in a lover's embrace."

Shaking his head slowly, he frowned and took another step closer. "We were not in a lover's embrace. In order for one to be in that position, both parties need to love each other. I assure you, I have no feelings for your maid."

"Yet you allowed her to kiss you, and you were clasping her shoulders."

"Actually, she had just barely pressed her mouth against mine when you walked in. The reason my hands were on her shoulders was because I tried to move her away. If you had entered the room only seconds later, I would have succeeded in ending the one-sided kiss and pushed her away." He sighed. "As I mentioned before, I don't want to do anything to lose your trust or friendship."

He glanced at the rose bushes again before looking at her. "May I?"

"You want to pluck a flower?"

"Yes, if it's all right with you."

She shrugged. "Go ahead."

He stepped to the white rose bush and plucked a rose, then to the yellow bush. Her heartbeat flipped wildly. Was he aware of what the colors symbolized? Most men in England knew what each color meant, but what of men in the United States? Dare she hope he was educated correctly?

He brought one of each flower back to her and presented them with a small bow. "I would very much like to give these to you, and I hope you will accept them with my sincere apology."

Hesitantly, she took them and lifted them to her nose to smell. Their scent had always relaxed her. "Thank you, Mr. Montgomery."

He moved closer and touched the petal of the white rose in a gentle stroke. "White stands for trust and loyalty, and the yellow rose is for friendship and compassion."

Gretta nearly fell to the ground. He had been educated. It surprised her that by knowing this about him, her respect for him grew.

"Indeed, they are. I'm surprised you knew that."

He winked. "My mother also loved rose bushes, and she taught me the meaning behind each color. That is how I know which rose I wanted to give you."

Why couldn't she tear herself away from his dreamy eyes? She was sinking fast, but she must start swimming or else she would drown.

"I commend you. Not many men in America have that knowledge." Gretta forced her legs to move as she walked past him into the garden a little further. He followed, but thankfully, not too close.

"Lady Brinley, will you accept my apology about what happened this morning and allow me to explain?"

She wanted to hear what he had to say, only because she prayed it would remove the image of him and Christine kissing from her mind. She kept her attention on the flowers, not wanting to get lost in his blue-eyed gaze again. "You may tell me now."

"I had brought up firewood to stock by the hearth while Christine cleaned out the ashes. Although I had seen the way she kept looking at me while we cleaned each room, I didn't think she would be so bold to steal a kiss."

Gretta's Gamble

Levi touched Gretta's arm, making her stop and look at him. He indeed appeared most sincere, but she couldn't become weak.

"She was the one who kissed me," he continued. "I didn't welcome her actions, nor was I about to participate. Her action was so quick that it caught me off guard. But the only reason I touched her was to move her away. Please forgive me for not being faster, because if I had, you would not have witnessed anything."

Gretta tilted her head, narrowing her gaze. "Are you trying to tell me you aren't attracted to lovely women?"

He chuckled softly. "What normal man wouldn't be? However, I'm not the kind of man who is always on the lookout for my next conquest."

Surprise washed over her, and she laughed. "Are you telling me you're not a rake?"

He grinned. "No, I'm not like that."

"I hope you don't mind me prying into your life, but I want you to tell me about the last woman who caught your fancy."

The humor on his face disappeared, and he turned away from her, continuing their leisurely walk. Perhaps she shouldn't have asked, but in order to get to know what kind of man he really was, she must know.

"Four months ago, I lived in Colorado. I met a very interesting woman, and I knew immediately, that she was the one I wanted to know more about. She acted as though she found me equally fascinating, which only encouraged me to pursue her. Not once did she oppose my attention, and I slowly gave her my heart. But when I discovered she had eyes for another man, it crushed me so much that I came to New York City, where I had been raised."

The sadness in his expression tore at Gretta's heart. It was clear that he told her the truth, only because she had felt that emotion after marrying Frederick. Although she wasn't in love with him, she had hoped that their marriage would eventually be the beginning of a true love between them. It was disheartening to discover how wrong she had been in assuming such an insane notion.

"I'm sorry I made you relive that heartache," she said softly. "Nobody should have to experience such a thing."

He stopped suddenly and turned toward her, which made her bump into him. His intense stare bore deep into her eyes.

"You have felt this way?" he asked.

She shrugged. "Mr. Montgomery, I would think most people have experienced that loss at least once in their lives."

"Will you tell me about your heartache?"

She really shouldn't share such personal information with a servant, yet since they first met, she found it easy to talk to him. His deep voice soothed her in some way. Not only that, but she needed more friends, and she desperately wanted Levi to be her friend.

"I can honestly say I was never in love," she began. "However, after Frederick started courting me, I had hoped we would fall in love after we were married. But I came to see that my dream would never come true. Frederick was more in love with hunting and gambling, and he was happier away from the manor—and his wife."

Confusion washed over Levi's expression. He touched her hand, and his warm, subtle gesture nearly had her melting to the ground and sighing aloud. But she stayed strong the best she could.

"Gretta, the man you married must have been a fool not to see the spectacular gift he had been offered. You are truly a fine woman who would make any normal man feel most fortunate to have you."

Tears of gratitude stung her eyes, and she quickly dropped her gaze, but when his gentle fingers stroked her chin and lifted her head, she had no choice but to stare into his eyes. Heavens, he was handsome, especially when he looked at her in that tender way. The rhythm of her heart quickened, and once again, she felt as though she was drowning. But this time, she didn't care. In fact, she hoped he would jump in and save her.

"You are the type of woman who should be treated like a queen," he continued.

"Levi, you shouldn't say such things. You don't know me well enough."

His gaze moved to her mouth, and her breathing accelerated. Although the idea of kissing him had tempted her on several occasions, she couldn't possibly follow through with her instincts. Especially, not out here where her servants could witness something so personal.

"Gretta, I would like it very much to know you better."

It was difficult, but she managed to step away from him before she let temptation rule her mind. "I appreciate your kindness, Levi, but we must not become too close. If you have been a servant before, you would know how gossip starts, and I don't wish to become the subject to such ridicule." She moved around him, putting distance between them. "It's bad enough that the servants are whispering about my missing brother as they try to play detective and speculate where he is, and why he is gone."

"Then let's stop those rumors." He walked beside her. "We need to find your brother. Please, Gretta, I cannot do this without you."

Sometimes she wished his words wouldn't make her feel so special, but it was nice to feel needed. She enjoyed feeling like she was important.

"I agree, Levi. We need to formulate a plan."

"Do you want to meet again tonight?"

Her heartbeat hammered as she looked into his eyes. "At the stable?"

He nodded. "Unless you want to meet some other place that is private."

It was on the tip of her tongue to invite him to her quarters. They didn't have to be anywhere near her bed, especially since she had a sofa and small table and chairs as well. The more she thought about the prospect of having him all to herself without the prying eyes of the servants, the more she liked the idea.

"After the servants retire for the night, sneak back into my quarters." Now that the words were out, she couldn't retract them. Then again, she didn't want to. The prospect of being alone with him again had excitement pumping through her body, faster than it ever had before.

Had she made a mistake by wanting their meeting *there*? The way his eyes changed colors, had her questioning her own sanity—and selfishness. Heaven help her, but she desired him, and she wanted to be the woman he thought her to be.

Indeed, this was an outlandish quest she was on, but for the life of her, she didn't want to stop it.

CHAPTER TEN

Levi paced the floor in his room. It was well past the time when servants should retire, but he didn't want to take any chances of being caught, especially by Conrad.

After Levi's visit with Gretta in the flower garden, he had returned to the manor only to meet the butler's suspicious scowl. The man's thin lips and judgmentally arched eyebrow let Levi know to be cautious. He wouldn't doubt the man stayed awake at night just seeing what kind of mischief was going on in the dark.

But the later the hour grew, the more he worried that Gretta might give up and retire for bed. He definitely wanted to see her tonight, and it had nothing to do with finding her brother.

Levi had already changed out of his footman's attire and wore the clothes that he first wore when she searched him out and found him in the stable the first day. She looked at him differently when he dressed like that. There was more desire in her pretty eyes. He also felt more like the Pinkerton agent he was while dressed that way and it gave him the confidence needed to find the thief. This case was already lasting too long, and he needed to end it soon, but with a positive outcome, of course.

He stepped quietly out of his room and closed the door, listening for any sounds that others were still awake. As he crept down the hallway, he walked as softly as his large boots would allow. A few times, the floor creaked, and he held his breath, praying that nobody would spot him.

The distance between his room and her quarters seemed longer, and he grew impatient. But he knew the importance of being discreet, and he didn't want to tarnish Gretta's reputation in any way. He felt closer to her since she shared that information about her husband. He wondered how many people really knew that about her. He hadn't heard negative whispers about the deceased Lord Brinley, and now Levi wondered if the reason why was because the man was never home enough for his servants to get to know him.

He hadn't lied when he told Gretta her husband must have been foolish. From what Levi knew about her, she was kind, giving, and had the sweetest heart. She was also very lovely, and her beauty lured him more than he was prepared for. He wouldn't mind seeing her passionate side, since he figured she would be lonely. And although he wondered what it would feel like to kiss her, he also didn't want her to think he would offer more since he wasn't the marrying kind, especially not after making that wager with his friends.

When he made it to her door without being spotted, he reached for the doorknob, but noticed the door wasn't fully closed. He hoped she was the one who had left it open for him so he didn't have to knock.

Cautiously, he slowly pushed the door open and stepped inside. In the first small room where her sofa, small table and chairs sat, the lamp had been turned down low, but toward her bedchamber, there was more light. He wondered if that was her subtle hint for him to go that way. He doubted she was the type of woman to seduce a man, although her maid would certainly do something like that.

He closed the door softly and moved toward her bedchamber. He prayed Gretta was really here and this wasn't a trap set by the alluring Christine. If the maid tried her wiles on him again, he would set her straight no matter how rude he was about it. He felt Gretta was closer to trusting him fully, and he didn't want to ruin it again.

As he entered her bedchamber, he noticed her sitting at her vanity table, staring at herself in the mirror. The shadows in the corner of the room played in her hair and face, making her appear more angelic, if that were possible. She had changed out of the dress she had worn when he saw her at supper, and although he knew she wouldn't wear her nightclothes, the light cream-colored material of her casual dress wasn't as thick as he was used to seeing. This was the type of dress a woman would wear if it was the middle of summer and the heat was melting her.

He enjoyed how her hair seemed browner, and how it hung provocatively over her shoulders and down her back. She wore no hair combs to keep the waves away from her face, and that in itself was quite alluring. Did she know how beautiful she was and how difficult this night would be as he concentrated on plans to find her brother? Would his mind stay on the true purpose of tonight's meeting, or would he want to sample her heart-shaped mouth?

He released a heavy sigh. He wasn't strong enough to resist her, even if she wasn't trying to tempt him.

Gretta spun around on her stool and faced him with wide eyes. Her hand rested on her bosom as she expelled a breath.

"Oh, you startled me," she said.

"Forgive me, I didn't mean to."

She stood and hastened her step toward him. "I had waited for you in the other room, but I grew weary of the wait."

He moved aside so she could pass him. Thankfully, she hadn't planned their meeting being in her bedchamber.

She walked to the lamp and turned it up before glancing toward the door. "I'm glad you closed the door." She looked over her shoulder at him. "Did anyone see you?"

He shook his head. "That was what took me so long. I wanted to make certain that the servants retired. I'm sorry I made you wait, but Conrad is very leery of me, and he watches me constantly. I didn't want him seeing me sneak up to your room."

"Don't be too harsh on Conrad. He is overprotective of me because of how Frederick treated me." She motioned her hand toward the table. He now could see there was a map opened with pencils and a magnifying glass.

"Would you like to come over here?"

What he would *like* and what he should do were two different things. But he would go with the latter since his *likes* were not going to find Charles.

As Levi moved toward her, he noticed her gaze slowly moving over his length. Once again, he was privileged to see the look of desire in her eyes, which softened her expression. He prayed the Lord helped him through this, because it would be difficult to resist a charming woman.

"While I waited for you," she said, "I outlined on this map places where my brother had been spotted. I'm not sure if I mentioned it, but my solicitor has had men out looking for Charles, but to no avail." She pointed to the map. "However, these are the locations they reported that my brother had been seen at."

Levi stopped beside her—but not too close—and studied the map. She smelled like flowers again, but he hadn't seen any of them in the room. How could he think straight like this?

"Do you know if these places you marked on the map of where your brother had been was *before* his disappearance, or was it *after*?"

She frowned. "I'm not certain. Part of me wanted to think that it was after he disappeared, only so it would make things easier to find him."

Levi moved away from Gretta long enough to retrieve the lamp and bring it back to the table. He leaned closer to the map and studied the markings.

"Which report was from the latest place Charles was spotted?"

Gretta leaned across him and pointed to a spot on the map. He held in a groan, wondering how he was going to keep from caressing her hair, or touching her in any way. He feared the slightest touch would make him want more.

"Someone saw Charles in this area by the Hudson River." She straightened, but still remained close. "When I heard this, I thought maybe Charles was hiding out in the slums, perhaps in disguise. Since you knew him, you probably recall how he loved to tease people by wearing different disguises."

Levi nodded, grateful for this bit of information since he didn't know Charles at all. "That is an excellent idea. If your brother knows he is in danger, then he would certainly disguise himself. I'm sure you are more aware of the different types of people he would dress up as."

Excitement sparkled in her eyes, brightening her face. "If I was in my brother's place, and I knew someone was after me, I would want the least amount of attention as possible."

"Charles wouldn't want anyone to think he came from upper class," Levi added.

"Exactly." She placed her hand on his forearm. "He would dress like a fisherman or someone that worked on the docks."

Enthusiasm rushed through Levi. Finally, they were getting somewhere. But why did she have to touch him because now he wanted to take her in his arms? But he wouldn't.

"Or your brother would dress like someone down on his luck. He might even beg for money since you and I both know those are the types of people the upper class tend to ignore."

She gasped and faced him, placing both hands on his chest. "Oh, Levi. That is a brilliant assumption. Charles would indeed do something like that."

Feeling her touch on his chest shot pleasure through him, and he lost his fight for control. By the way she stared into his eyes with such admiration, and how his body buzzed with awareness, he knew he wouldn't be able to stop the inevitable.

Silence filled the air, except for his choppy breathing. But he noticed that her breathing had become ragged, as well. Did she feel the spark jumping back and forth between them? Yet she hadn't moved away, nor did she remove her hands from his chest.

Slowly, he slid his arms around her, splaying his palms on her back as he gently guided her closer. The different emotions registering on her face ranged from surprise, curiosity, and finally yearning and acceptance.

Her gaze dropped to his mouth, and he knew just as the sun would rise tomorrow, that he was going to kiss her tonight. That kind of knowledge was dangerous yet exhilarating.

She opened her mouth as if she wanted to speak, but no words came out. Instead, her tongue darted out and swept across her raspberry lips.

He held in a groan. That was all the encouragement he needed. He lowered his head slowly, giving her the time to tell him no. Once again, no words came from her throat to stop him.

The moment he reached her mouth, he brushed his lips against hers. Just like a rose petal, her lips were delicately soft.

Gretta held her breath, and at first, her body was stiff, but within seconds, she released a low groan and melted in his arms. He tightened his embrace to keep her from crumbling to the floor, but it also made it more comfortable to kiss her.

As much as he wanted to show her the wild sensations rushing through him right now, he took the kiss slow, still fearing she would find reason to stop his enjoyment. He had wondered if kissing her would be passionate, and now he knew it exceeded his expectations.

Another squeak released from her throat as she slid her hands up his chest and circled her arms around his neck. This very movement turned the kiss hotter, and more passionate. He couldn't tighten his hold around her for fear of breaking her ribs, but because of the way she pressed against him and met his kiss with such eagerness, he realized she was indeed experiencing the same sensations as he was.

He never wanted this to end, yet if it didn't end soon, he feared he would become the despicable rake she loathed. He wasn't like the other men who took advantage of a woman's loneliness, but in a sense, he was lonely as well and sought the same recognition that she searched for.

When he felt her fingers running through his hair, he let out a pleasurable moan, loving that she wasn't afraid to touch him. In turn, he found her silky locks and enjoyed stroking her hair before cupping her head and holding it while they kissed.

The grandfather clock in the hall struck the late hour of one and brought him out of the clouds that her kiss had sent him to. Although he didn't want to do anything to ruin the moment, he also knew that if they didn't stop now, they might do something they would regret later.

Gretta's Gamble

He slowed the kiss, and soon he felt her pull away. As he peered into her dazed eyes and saw the excitement still displayed, his heart soared. She smiled and dropped her hands. He was hesitant to leave her side so he caressed her cheek.

Gretta cleared her throat. "I... um, I don't know what to say."

He grinned. "I, too, find myself speechless." He swept his thumb over her bottom lip. "I sure hope you aren't seeking an apology, because I'm not sorry for kissing you like that. I enjoyed every second of it."

Her face reddened. "No, there is no reason to apologize. I enjoyed it as well."

Levi chuckled lightly. "Your nearness distracted me in the worst way, and seeing the enthusiasm in your eyes and having you touch my chest was my undoing."

"Then perhaps it is I who should apologize."

He shook his head. "Don't you dare."

She smiled shyly. "Then I won't."

She was absolutely adorable, and he couldn't help himself from kissing her lips one last time, but briefly. When he pulled away, the look of disappointment was in her expression. It was comical, but he wouldn't laugh.

"Well, Gretta, I think we will know where to start looking for your brother now." He motioned his head toward the map on the table. "Should we start our journey tomorrow?"

She blinked a few times as if trying to regain her bearings. He was happy to know his kiss had knocked her senseless, since he felt similar emotions.

"Oh, no. Tomorrow is out of the question. I have a prior engagement. Tomorrow night I will be attending a ball at the Weatherly estate."

Disappointed, he frowned. "You can't get out of it?"

"No. I'm trying to prove to society that I'm not a countess who is sulking because my husband died. I need to make an appearance, but after that, we can start looking for Charles."

He shrugged and sighed. "Well, as much as I would rather have you all to myself as quickly as possible, I suppose one more day won't hurt."

Gretta patted his chest. "Now Levi, you will still go with me as my footman when we look for Charles, so although we will be together, you must continue to act as my servant."

Levi gritted his teeth. He had one day to figure out another way, because being her servant was out of the question. Hopefully, he would think of something clever before they were ready to leave.

Gretta's Gamble

CHAPTER ELEVEN

Her maid had already left the room, but Gretta still messed with her hair that had been loosely coiled and pinned at the top of her head. She plucked the tendrils near her ears, fixing them to fall perfectly. There really was no reason to look her best at the Weatherly's ball tonight because she wasn't trying to impress anyone. She just wanted society to know she wasn't cowering in her manor after her husband disgraced the Brinley name by nearly making them penniless because of his insistent gambling.

It was difficult for her to appear joyful in front of those people she knew in New York City, only because she knew they looked down on her. Many matrons had hinted that Gretta find herself a wealthy husband quickly, but she just didn't want to follow their rules. If she learned anything from her marriage, it was that she could function just fine without a man.

Then again, after the passionate kiss she shared with Levi last night, she realized she was indeed missing something. She missed the intimacy that she should have had with Frederick—the tender affection she longed for with Levi.

Although she still wanted to return to England, she wondered if Levi would come with her. Nobody in the *ton's* circles would have to know he was her footman. He could be anyone he wanted to be in England, she would make certain of it. Of course, she now held ideas about him being a good husband, but she didn't want to force it on him.

Sighing, she ran her palms down her white gown trimmed with blue ribbon on the sleeves, the hem, and matching sash around her waist. As she studied her appearance, she realized she needed jewelry. She reached for the jewelry box and opened it. She loved the sapphire necklace and earbobs. This was her favorite because it had belonged to her mother.

Seeing all the other jewels that Frederick had given her since they were married made her heart hurt. The trinkets were purchased those time when she complained about him being gone so much. Yet now she wondered if the jewelry was worth anything. Why would he spend money on real gems when that money was used for gambling?

However, the ruby necklace he had given her on their one-year anniversary, was certainly real, only because she had Conrad examine it since he was familiar with jewels. But Frederick had told her to keep it in a safe place. Perhaps the man thought he might be tempted to sell it to pay for his gambling habits. That was probably the reason she didn't like to wear it very often now that he was dead.

In fact, the first time Charles had seen her wear the necklace, he even instructed her not to flaunt it in public. His reasoning was because of Frederick's gambling problem and that others might think he had swindled it off some man he cheated. At the time, she had listened to her brother. Now she wondered if he was the one who had stolen it, instead. But that didn't explain how Frederick was able to give it to her.

A knock came upon her door, startling her. Her carriage must be ready to take her to the ball tonight but why was it so early? She hadn't planned on arriving for another hour.

She walked out of her bedchamber and into the sitting room of her quarters. When she opened the door, it surprised her to see Levi carrying a tray of teacups and a tea kettle, wearing his footman uniform.

His gaze swept over her, and his smile widened. She loved the way his eyes sparkled like gems.

"Good evening, Lady Brinley," he said in a voice that was louder than she thought it should be.

"Good evening, Mr. Montgomery."

He motioned his head toward the tea service. "I have brought up your tea, as requested."

Gretta's Gamble

What was he talking about? She narrowed her eyes, wondering what game he played with her. But then he winked, and she knew.

Trying not to laugh, she straightened her shoulders and opened the door wider. "Yes, thank you, Mr. Montgomery. You are right on time. Please, set it on my table."

"As you wish."

His gaze stayed on her as he entered. Her heart fluttered with happiness. She was glad he came to see her before she left for the ball.

She glanced down the hall and didn't see any of the other servants, so slowly pushed the door almost closed but she left it ajar just in case. He set the tea service tray on the table and turned toward her. Since the table was out of view from the hall, she knew nobody would see her or Levi unless they came completely into the room.

"You look lovely tonight, Lady Brinley."

Her heart warmed by the way his gaze slid over her in leisure, and especially the way his smile grew.

She hurried to him and threw her arms around his neck. Immediately, he took her into a tight embrace.

"Thank you for coming to see me," she whispered.

"Serving your tea was the only excuse I could think of to hold you for a few minutes." He kissed her forehead. "I haven't been able to get you off my mind since last night."

She sighed heavily, learning against him more. "I have been the same way today. I couldn't concentrate on anything."

He bent his head and brushed his lips across hers before trailing kisses over her chin to her neck. "I can't wait to be with you tomorrow while we search for Charles."

"Yes." She closed her eyes, tilting her head back.

"But I don't want to go as your footman."

"Umm," she muttered enjoying the intimate moment with him.

"Instead," he continued, "will you allow me to go as your uncle or even a cousin?"

His deep voice comforted her, and she wasn't fully comprehending what he was asking. But at this point, she would agree to anything, as long as he kept kissing her. She didn't even care if she was extremely late for the ball. "All right... Anything you say, Levi."

His mouth finally covered hers and the kiss was just as exhilarating as the one they shared last night. She loved that her body thrilled in the attention he showed her.

She didn't know how much time had passed—two minutes, two hours—but she couldn't stop kissing him. She never wanted to stop. But the giggles from her maids down the hall broke the passionate moment. Gretta groaned and pulled away, looking into Levi's eyes. His expression was filled with disappointment, just as she knew hers was.

He released her and she smoothed her palms down the front of her gown, hoping there were no noticeable wrinkles. But he touched his fingers to her lips and winked.

"Let me give you a bit of advice," he whispered. "Don't leave the room until the swelling goes down in your lips. If your servants notice, they will know you have been kissing someone."

She gasped and placed her hand over her mouth.

"Enjoy your party tonight, but don't miss me too much."

She loved his teasing grin as he walked out of her room and closed the door. On weak legs, she moved to the sofa and sat.

Her body still tingled from being in his arms, and she knew that she couldn't fight the emotion any longer. As soon as they found Charles, she would move back to England and take Levi with her. She just hoped he would agree.

The ninety minutes it took from the time Levi left her room and when arriving at the Weatherly's ball, was tedious. She hadn't wanted to leave her quarters for fear that the servants would see her swollen lips and speculate who she had been kissing. But she also didn't want to attend a ball by herself. Loneliness had become her companion since her marriage to Frederick, and now that Levi had awakened her emotions, she realized that being by herself wasn't what she wanted.

Gretta's Gamble

As she entered the grand manor, she kept her chin up and promised herself she would only stay for an hour and then leave. Then she would have at least accomplished her first goal in letting society see that she wasn't sulking like an injured child.

She nodded greetings to familiar faces before stopping to chat briefly with Mr. and Mrs. Weatherly, giving them compliments about their beautiful estate and the furnishings inside the manor. Mr. Weatherly had made a fortune owning and breeding racehorses. It surprised Gretta that one could make so much money just in racing horses.

Time passed slowly, and she was tired of seeing the pitiful looks of sympathy people gave her, as well as haughty glances from the wives of rich husbands who knew Gretta was not going to find a wealthy husband, mainly because all she had worth marrying for was a nice estate and a few servants.

As she stood in the corner of the ballroom, sipping her punch, her mind wandered back to Levi. He had never made her feel unworthy. Just the opposite, in fact. His words mixed with the way he looked at her made her feel like a queen. How many women at this party could say the same about their husbands or beaus?

When should she make her excuses and head home? She searched for a timepiece and when she found one, noticed she had only been at the party thirty minutes. Only thirty more to go.

"Pardon me, but I don't believe we have been properly introduced."

The man's voice brought her out of the thoughts tumbling in her head and she turned to look at the gentleman beside her. At first, all she saw was Levi when she peered at him, but then shook away the daydream as she studied the handsome stranger. Yet he looked so much like Levi, it was remarkable. Same eye color, same slicked back hair, and exactly the same muscular build. But this man was dressed so eloquently, and he wore a mustache.

She blinked several times, not believing what she saw. There couldn't possibly be two men that were so similar in appearance. But she was certainly not seeing correctly. Either that or she had been thinking of Levi so much lately that she saw him in everyone.

He bowed slightly and took her hand, brought it up to his mouth and brushed a gentle kiss on her knuckles. His blue eyes sparkled in that familiar way that made her think he was in a teasing mood.

"Let me introduce myself," he continued as he straightened. "I'm Leviticus Staton Montgomery, co-owner of the railroad and a member of the stock exchange."

She must be dreaming, but that was Levi's voice, and those were his amazing eyes, and his very kissable lips. However, her mind was hesitant to believe, and no words were forthcoming as she stared at this incredible man.

"But you, Lady Brinley, may call me Levi." He winked, kissing her hand again but lingering.

Her stomach flip-flopped as butterflies danced in her chest. Indeed, this was really happening. "What... I don't understand." She ran her gaze over his attire, wondering where he had found such an expensive suit.

"Were you aware," he said in a low voice, "that Uncle Reginald still has suits from when he was younger and more robust?" He chuckled. "I wouldn't have believed it, until he mentioned it earlier today when I was visiting with him."

Her mind opened and she recalled when she was younger, and her uncle had been muscular and was sought after by all the women searching for a wealthy husband. But she didn't know her relative had kept his clothes from all those years ago.

She dropped her gaze to Levi's tempting mouth. "But I don't think my uncle had fake facial hair."

Levi laughed, and a few couples turned to look their way. She didn't care. Let them stare at the most handsome man at the ball.

"Actually, that is another tidbit I discovered about him today. He was a man who had many personas, and the outfits that went with each identity." He smoothed a finger over his mustache. "And this came from his collection."

She sighed heavily and shook her head. "Why didn't I know?"

Levi shrugged. "Sadly, such is the life of a man who wears many disguises. They don't tell their secrets to women, especially if they are related."

She grinned. "And pray tell, why are you at the ball? In fact, how did you get inside without a proper invitation?"

He took her hand and hooked it over his arm as he led her away from the wall. "It seems that nobody checks the yard for intruders." He arched an eyebrow. "And since the Weatherly's keep their servants doing other things, nobody saw me squeeze through the hedges and come the back way."

Amazed, all Gretta could do was shake her head. "Levi, I cannot believe you are really here, and dressed like *that*."

He smiled. "I think if I would have come dressed as the footman, the Weatherly's would have put me to work." He shrugged. "And if I came in my own clothes, they would have tossed me out to the stables."

"Oh, Levi." Her heartbeat hammered so happily she could scarcely breathe. "You don't know how much I wanted you to be here. I have thought of you nonstop since arriving. I didn't want to come to the ball alone, but that was my only choice."

His expression softened, becoming more serious. "And you're not alone and you can enjoy yourself for the rest of the night."

"But Levi? What if someone at the party asks you about being a co-owner of a railroad and owning stock? Surely they will see through your lie."

"Perhaps, or maybe I will be charming enough to make them believe."

She stopped, which made him turn and face her. "Is your real name really Leviticus Staton Montgomery?"

"Upon my word, it is the truth. My parents named me after a book in the Bible, but when I was old enough, I made everyone call me Levi."

"If anything, you are a very interesting man, Levi. People will be sucked in by your charm."

He waggled his eyebrows. "That is what I'm hoping for."

"And if they ask how I know you, what should I say?"

"You can tell them I'm your American cousin."

"But Levi, I don't have American relatives."

He leaned toward her ear. "Nobody needs to know that." He straightened. "Besides, since this is how I will be able to travel with you tomorrow, people need to get to know me somehow, in case they see us together in the upcoming days."

All sense of humor disappeared, and her chest tightened. "Do you think it will take that long to find Charles?"

He nodded. "It may take longer. We can only pray to find your brother faster." He lifted her hand to his mouth again and kissed her knuckles. "Now, let us mingle for a little while longer and then I will take you home."

"Yes, that is a splendid idea."

Although she wore white elbow gloves, the feel of his hot breath on her hand continued to send tingles up her spine. She feared she would sigh aloud with contentment, and everyone would hear her, but the truth was, Levi Montgomery made her happier than she had ever been, and heaven help her, but she wanted everyone to know. Sadly, this was something she must keep to herself.

She headed in a different direction than where Levi had gone. Mingling wasn't one of her strong suits, but she would try, only because it would make time pass by quicker. But just as she realized, most people didn't want to socialize with her, and she knew it was because of Frederick.

When she reached the other side of the ballroom without seeing anyone who looked like they wanted to talk, she turned and moved in a different direction. Faces soon became a blur, and she stopped admiring the gowns of most of the women.

Inwardly, she groaned. Why couldn't she just leave now?

She stopped and studied the couples dancing, looking for Levi. He would surely ask some fortunate woman for a dance. It only took a second before she spotted him, but she was relieved to see that his dance partner was Mrs. Weatherly, a woman who was old enough to be his mother.

Satisfied that he wasn't trying to charm a lovely *younger* woman, Gretta headed toward the refreshment table. She needed another drink. As she neared, a man stood with two women as they chatted, and Gretta felt she had met him recently. He looked awfully familiar, but she couldn't figure out where she had seen him. After all, she had kept to her estate, and had only taken the coach when she went to find her brother at the prison.

Suddenly, her mind opened, and she saw this man at the prison, dressed in the guard's attire. Yet if he was merely a guard, would he be invited to such a pristine ball? And more importantly, would he run in the same circles as Mr. and Mrs. Weatherly?

Gretta quickly stepped away from the table, but not far enough to be hidden. She tried listening to the conversation he had with the two women. What was his name? He had an odd name, not recalling ever hearing it before.

His name sprang to her mind. Felix Chappell. She had given him Uncle Reginald's banknotes to pay Levi's bail to get him out of that terrible prison.

Cautiously, she moved toward the table again, this time she kept her side or back to the man in case he recognized her. Thankfully, she could hear their conversation a little better now, and it sounded as if he was trying to charm the ladies because they giggled like schoolgirls. And then she heard the name one of the women called him. Mr. Halverson.

Gretta frowned. Had she been mistaken about this man? Or did he have two identities? There was only one way for her to know.

She turned toward the table and waited until the servant poured her another glass of punch. Gretta watched Mr. Chappell, waiting for him to look at her. When after a few moments and he didn't, she took her drink and stepped closer to the trio. Finally, the man glanced at her, but just as he had moved his gaze back to the women, it snapped and rested on Gretta. She gave him a smile before taking a sip of her drink.

He said something to the ladies before moving toward Gretta. He gave her a nod of recognition.

"Good evening, Lady Brinley. How nice it is to see you again."

"It is nice to see you as well, Mr. Chappell... or is it Mr. Halverson?" She tilted her head. "I am pretty good at remembering names, and I know you told me your name was Felix Chappell." She pointed to the women who were walking back into the ballroom. "Or was it them you lied to instead?"

He sighed heavily and folded his arms. "If you must know, I'm working undercover."

She hiccupped a laugh. "That sounds like something a liar would say."

"Truly, Lady Brinley." His voice lowered. "I'm a Pinkerton agent and I'm here using a different name. My name is Felix Chappell, but I was working undercover at the prison, as well. As an agent, we dress to the character we play."

She took another sip, not knowing if she could believe him or not. "So, if you were working undercover at the prison, I believe you owe me money. After all, I did pay you to release Mr. Montgomery, did I not?"

He scowled. "You did, but... I gave the money to the warden since that was who gets the payment to release prisoners."

She didn't know how to prove it, but she knew without a doubt this man was lying to her. But there was no use arguing. It was better just to drop the subject. "Fine, then I hope you have a good evening."

He nodded. "And you as well."

He marched into the ballroom, and she turned back to the refreshment table. The cookies smelled delightful, but she wasn't in the mood for treats now. She still wanted to go home. When would it be time? Hadn't she shown these people she wasn't going to hide from her husband's problems?

Gretta's Gamble

Gretta finished the drink and gave the servant the empty glass. Slowly, she moved back into the ballroom, looking for the most handsome man she had ever seen. Immediately, she saw him talking to another man. Their heads were bent close together as if trying to talk in private.

She moved toward him, but not even halfway there, Levi pulled away and she could see the other man better. She stopped suddenly as confusion filled her more than before. Why was Levi and Mr. Chappell chatting as though they were longtime friends?

Mr. Chappell had mentioned that Pinkerton agents dress as the character they portray for their undercover assignment. Did that mean…

She held her breath. No. She wouldn't believe it. Levi Montgomery could not be a Pinkerton agent as well. But it certainly explained a few things about him.

Her skull pounded as she began piecing together everything that had happened since meeting Levi. She hoped she was wrong, but she had the sinking suspicion that *she* was his undercover assignment.

The twisting in her stomach let her know that she might empty the contents inside any minute now. She certainly couldn't do that here.

She hurried around people, making her way toward one of the side doors. She would find a plant or piece of grass out in the yard to regurgitate.

The room started spinning, but thankfully, she made it outside and found a shaded tree just in time. She bent over and let everything come forth. For a moment, she didn't even care if it touched her gown. All she wanted to do was return home and go to bed, whether she slept or not, she didn't want to feel the crushing blow of betrayal.

Gretta took a few deep breaths, and when she felt that she was fine, she straightened and wiped her gloved hand across her mouth. Knowing that it was now on her glove, she removed both and tossed them in the bushes.

Placing a hand to her stomach, she dared to move out of shadows, but took her time. She was in no rush, even though she must get Levi to confess his part in the charade somehow.

She stopped before leaving the shadows and peered toward the manor. A man moved across the patio quickly before disappearing behind the structure. Once again, pain pierced through her skull and created havoc in her stomach. Yet it wasn't Levi or Mr. Chappell this time.

Indeed, she must not be well because she thought for sure that she saw… Frederick.

The dizziness that had threatened her earlier came back, and this time, she couldn't fight it. As she fell to the grass, she was certain that she had just seen her dead husband.

Gretta's Gamble

CHAPTER TWELVE

Levi moved away from Felix as he scanned the crowded ballroom. It had surprised him to see his Pinkerton friend, but it was a good thing since Levi was able to update Felix on what had transpired in the search for Charles. Felix agreed that Gretta's brother was probably living somewhere by the docks and in disguise. Thankfully, Pinkerton agents were trained to look for people who had stolen another's identity.

The hour was late, and he knew Gretta wanted to get back home. He had to admit that he didn't like the life of going from one party to the next like most wealthy couples did. However, he wanted to dance at least once with Gretta before they left.

After scanning the room, and not seeing the only beautiful woman at this gathering, he immediately became worried. He doubted she had returned home yet—at least not without telling him. Maybe she waited for him on the patio. After all, the ballroom was very stuffy.

Levi nodded to people as he passed by. He couldn't wait to have another moment with Gretta before returning home. Of course, he would have to be careful with his disguise. It would look a little odd to have his cousin kissing him, though not uncommon. He grinned. It was still the perfect cover for them to be seen together.

Lanterns lined the garden area. His gaze wandered over the yard. A sudden movement from a nearby tree caught his attention. He was positive it was Gretta. He took a few steps onto the grass, just as her body collapsed lifeless to the ground.

He ran toward her. No one even noticed the fallen woman, as they were too caught up in their own uppity lives to care. Levi fell to his knees and scooped her head into his arms. The rise and fall of her breathing indicated that she was alive, yet by the paleness of her face, he could tell something was wrong.

"Gretta." He lightly patted her cheeks. "Gretta, wake up." He took his hand and fanned her face. "Sweetheart, wake up."

Gretta's eyes twitched, then slowly opened. Her glossy-eyed look confirmed that she was still not fully conscious. He put her head down softly and stood. Levi needed to get her to the coach to rest. He lifted her into his arms, and she softly moaned.

"Frederick," she mumbled.

It broke his heart that she would call for her deceased husband and not him, especially when she had told him she never loved the man. Levi tried not to let it bother him as he carried her toward the parked coaches. A few of the coachmen stood at attention, staring at him in shock.

"Gilbert." Levi called out to Gretta's driver. "Open the door."

Gilbert looked at him strangely, but then he recognized Gretta in his arms and quickly opened the coach's door.

"Go fetch some water," Levi instructed. "She has fainted."

Gilbert rushed toward the coach house while Levi settled her inside the vehicle, with her head on the seat. He knew sitting her up too soon would only make her faint again. He loosened the blue sash around her waist, since that was really the only proper thing he could do. He lifted her feet slightly, to allow the blood to flow better through her body. Levi remembered his grandfather giving him instructions when he was younger. If he hadn't became a Pinkerton, a physician would probably have been his career.

Levi removed her shoes and rubbed her feet. He watched her chest as it rose and fell in a normal rhythm. Maybe it was something she ate that caused her to lose consciousness.

"Gretta," he said again. "Can you open your eyes?"

Gretta's Gamble

Her eyes fluttered again, and then slowly opened. This time he could see confusion written on her expression as her gaze darted around the dark coach.

"Sir," Gilbert said, "here is some water."

Levi took the cup and moved closer to her. Gretta scrambled to sit upright.

"Gretta, don't move too quickly," Levi said. "Drink this."

Her gaze stopped on him, and she blinked as if she was trying to focus.

"What happened?" She sipped the water.

"I saw you collapse underneath a tree." He touched her head, and she shrieked back a bit. He continued his advances on her to withdraw a piece of grass from her hair. He held it out for her to observe. "How do you feel?"

She looked down at her bare feet and wiggled her toes. "I swear I came with shoes."

"I slipped them off. I needed to get your blood moving again. Did you eat something that disagreed with you?"

She took another sip of the water then handed it back to Gilbert.

"No. Actually, a lot of things weren't agreeing with me tonight." She met the driver's gaze. "You can return the cup, then I want to go home."

"Yes, Lady Brinley." Gilbert nodded and rushed away.

"I don't understand," Levi replied.

"I saw you talking with someone." She cleared her throat and adjusted on the seat. "It was the guard at the prison, Mr. Chappell. What I found curious was that you both acted as though you knew each other well."

Levi's breath caught in his throat as panic filled him. Out of all the people at the party, why did she notice Felix? With Gretta under distress at the prison, he was sure she wouldn't remember anyone's faces. She was certainly more observant than he gave her credit for.

"Mr. Chappell recognized me," Levi lied. "He was concerned that I was there to lose miserably at a card game again. Some of the men were planning something for later."

"Mr. Montgomery." Gretta squared her shoulders. She had that sharp tone in her voice, reminding him that she was his employer. "Mr. Chappell told me he was a Pinkerton agent and that he dresses the part when he is undercover, like all Pinkertons do." She threw him a glare. "Something isn't right, I can feel it. I'm believing our meeting was indeed set up."

"Gretta, let me explain—"

"You absolutely will, Mr. Montgomery. The lies stop now. If I'm not satisfied with your explanation, I'm kicking you out on your ear, and I will find my brother myself." She folded her arms.

Even though he was now caught in this scheme, he couldn't help but admit he loved the way she looked. Her hair was messed up from the fall, and a little dirt smudged her nose, but she was absolutely adorable.

Levi released a heavy sigh. He must tell her everything, and hopefully in return, she wouldn't leave him on the side of the road.

"The truth?" he asked.

"Don't you think I deserve the truth?"

"You do." He paused, wondering how to begin this. From the corner of his eye, he noticed Gilbert approaching. "May I ride with you as I explain?"

Gretta nodded.

"Gilbert, my horse is in the stable. Would you bring him to me? Let the stableboy know the horse is for Leviticus Montgomery."

Confusion filled the driver's face as his gaze jumped between Gretta and Levi. Although the moment wasn't comical, Levi found it amusing that the driver hadn't seen through his disguise.

Gretta nodded to the man. "It's fine, Gilbert. Do as Mr. Montgomery requests."

Gilbert turned and left them alone again. Hopefully he wouldn't figure out that the man helping Lady Brinley was really the footman.

Gretta's Gamble

"All right, you better start talking." Gretta retightened her blue sash around her waist.

"I am a Pinkerton agent."

"And I'm your assignment, right?" She shook her head. "I can't believe I fell for your lies."

"Will you let me explain? Stop putting words in my mouth, please. I have my reasons as to why I'm in here."

"Fine. Pardon my interruption. You may continue." She sat back, folding her arms.

"I'm not Charles' friend." Her mouth dropped open, and part of him died inside. This was what he hated about being an agent.

"Then how did you know about my cat?"

"My colleagues have been following this case for a year now. They knew about you and Charles. I actually met your brother not long after I was put on the case. He tends to run at the mouth when he has drunk too much whiskey. I didn't have enough evidence to arrest him at that time. If I had, I would have never involved you."

Her eyes watered, and she blinked rapidly. "Do you and the other Pinkerton agents believe Charles has stolen something?"

"A wealthy widow, Mrs. Kensington, lives in Yonkers, and her prized necklace was stolen about a year ago. We asked many people who had been at her social gathering that evening, and although we had a few suspects, Charles was the one who was mentioned the most. There were more thefts around that time frame, and they all lead toward your brother. But when we couldn't find proof, the case grew cold. Mrs. Kensington contacted Allan Pinkerton and had more people put on it, but we couldn't find your brother anywhere. So, Felix Chappell and I thought up a plan. I was going to be your brother in jail since he works undercover at the prison on occasion. I knew you would eventually figure out that I wasn't Charles, so I was hoping we could help each other in finding your brother." Levi paused. "That's it. The truth."

A tear slid down her cheek. "Why do the men in my life have to lie to me? The only one who has never lied is Uncle Reginald."

"Gretta," Levi said, putting his hand on top of hers. "It was not my plan to hurt you. It never was. It also wasn't my plan to have feelings for you."

She yanked her hand away. Outside he heard a horse approaching them. Gilbert was back.

"I want you out of my carriage," she demanded. "I need time to process this information."

"I understand." Levi stepped out of the vehicle. "But the longer we wait to find Charles, the harder it will be. I'm only hoping it's not too late already."

"Levi, did he really steal that lady's necklace?"

"We are only going on speculation right now. But think of this… If he didn't steal it, why is he in hiding?" Levi closed the door to the coach.

Gretta scooted toward the window as he mounted his horse. She opened the window and looked at him.

"I haven't seen Charles since right after Frederick died," she mumbled. "We were always close, but I never knew him to steal. Yes, he loved to gamble, but he was much better at it than Frederick."

"The widow's necklace is worth a lot of money. The cut of the ruby is the most exquisite. Mrs. Kensington said it has been passed down through her family for years."

Gretta's eyebrows raised. "Rubies?"

"Yes. It's a heart-shaped ruby necklace." He kicked the sides of his horse to move it along the side of her coach.

He tried to study her expression while guiding his horse to keep from running into anything as they traveled. But her expression told him what he needed to know. She had seen the necklace before.

She turned and lifted the window, closing it. His chest tightened. One way or another, he needed her help. At this point, if she refused to help him, the case would turn cold again and there wasn't anything he could do.

Gretta's Gamble

* * * *

The bouncing of the carriage made Gretta's headache worse. But returning to her bedchambers and crying her eyes out was the only thing on her mind, even if it would make her head hurt worse. Returning to England and running away from all this drama was still an option.

Should she tell Levi about her necklace? It couldn't be the one that was stolen, but how many heart-shaped ruby necklaces were out there? Frederick told her the necklace was an heirloom in his family and he wanted her to have it. But if the piece of jewelry was the same, had Frederick stolen it instead of Charles? And how could she prove it?

Her first thought was to give Levi the necklace so that he would be out of her life. But then, Charles would still be gone. Sadly, Levi had been correct in saying that they needed each other.

Now that the Weatherly's ball was over, first thing in the morning, she and Levi would begin their search, and during that time, she would not let him touch her. Not ever again.

Had his charm been a lie as well, even if he told her it wasn't? But it didn't matter. He should have known not to kiss a lonely, unsuspecting widow who longed for a man's love. But she certainly wasn't going to get it from Levi Montgomery.

When the coach stopped in front of the manor, she didn't wait for anyone to help her out. She swung the door open and prepared to leave, but suddenly, Levi was in front of her, taking her hand and assisting her. She allowed it, but once her feet were firmly planted on the ground, she yanked away.

She took three steps toward the manor but stopped. Tears stung her eyes, but she refused to shed them in front of him.

Taking a deep breath, she tried to gain courage to face him. Finally, she spun around. He stood very near, and the sadness coating his expression nearly shattered her.

"Be ready first thing in the morning so we can find my brother."

He sighed and his mouth lifted in a small smile. "Thank you, Gretta. We'll find him, I know it."

"We will, and as soon as we do, I'll make you eat your words when Charles tells you he didn't steal that necklace. Then, at least I can feel good about knowing the stress of the situation isn't making me insane."

He arched an eyebrow. "Gretta, you aren't going insane."

She rolled her eyes. "I must be, because the reason I passed out at the party was that I thought I saw Frederick. I know my husband isn't alive, yet I saw him." She shook her head.

He reached out his hand to touch her. "Gretta, I don't think—"

"Don't," she snapped, taking a step back. "You will never have that privilege again."

Without waiting for Levi to respond, or looking upon his sad expression, she hurried straight to her bedchambers, holding up her hand to her wide-eyed maids to leave her be. Letting her frustration control her actions, she slammed the door shut. She ran to her bed and fell onto the comfortable pillows. Now, she wouldn't hold back the tears. She didn't think she could even if she tried since they were already spilling down her cheeks.

She closed her eyes, hoping her temples would stop pounding like a drum. Her mind opened again, and she was back at the party. As clear as day, she saw the figure of the man rushing along the patio toward the manor. Her heartbeat accelerated as though she was witnessing it all over again. The man's features were those of Frederick's, she was sure of it. Had she seen a ghost?

The person wore a tan suit, much like what Frederick would have worn when he went out to the horse races. As the man passed by the lanterns, she had noticed his wavy blond hair... just like Frederick's. *No.* Her chest tightened with uncertainty. Frederick was dead and buried deep in the ground at the cemetery. She wasn't insane—just stressed.

Gretta rolled off her pillows and wiped the wetness from her face. She stood, slipped out of her gown, and hung it over the chair in the room. Gretta opened the closet door and reached to the top shelf, pulling down a large jewelry box. As she opened the lid and looked down at the sparkling heart-shaped ruby necklace, her breath caught in her throat.

Frederick told her the necklace was his grandmother's and that he wanted Gretta to have it. Besides her wedding band, this was the most expensive thing he ever gave her. For now, she would hide this from Levi and not say anything about it until after Charles was found and the accusations against him were dropped. He was *not* the thief. If anything, Frederick had been since he was the one with the jewelry.

Gretta returned the necklace to the top shelf in the closet and placed some bonnets on top to hide it. Now that she thought about it, she was sure Levi had been looking for the necklace that day she caught him in her room. Everything made sense now. Why had she been so naïve? Then again, she wasn't used to a handsome man telling her she was pretty, or looking at her as though he desired her.

Once she proved Charles' innocence, she would convince him to move back to England with her and start a new life. There was nothing for her here any longer.

* * * *

The morning arrived too soon, and by the feel of her heavy eyelids, she wondered if she had even slept. Gretta splashed cold water on her face to wake herself up. Her dreams were filled with ghosts and lies. Today she must put it all behind her. Her mind should be alert if she wanted to find Charles. He was out there somewhere. She knew her brother had done regretful things in his life, but she doubted her brother would sink so low as to become a thief.

Gretta dressed in a light peach-colored day dress, with a round neckline. She wore a matching bonnet, as what was fashionable, even if she would rather not have to wear one. The weather was still cool in the morning, so she donned a light tan Spencer jacket.

She looked at herself in the mirror, hoping that the bags under her eyes weren't noticeable to others. No matter how hard it would be working with Levi, she had to push her feelings aside and focus on Charles.

Gretta moved down the stairs slowly, watching the maids as they straightened items in the foyer. As she glanced around the foyer, she realized how terribly lonely her life had become. At her age, she should have already bore children, at least a few. If only things had been different between her and Frederick. Perhaps the stress of seeing all the happy couples at the ball last night, along with realizing Levi and Mr. Chappell were friends, was what caused her to see Frederick's ghost.

"Lady Brinley," Conrad said as he rounded the corner at the same time she did. "I was told you had plans for today, but you never mentioned anything to me." His gaze wandered over her dress. "You aren't going riding in that, are you?"

"Conrad, I'm going into town for a while." She paused in thought. Conrad had been with her and Frederick for a very long time, and he would know if she was lying. And truly, he had only been trying to protect her which was what made him so curious.

"Should I get Mrs. Patterson to accompany you?"

"No. I have asked Mr. Montgomery to take me into town," she replied.

Conrad's expression tightened. Immediately, she recalled Levi telling her that the butler didn't like him very well. Of course, ever since Conrad noticed Frederick's treatment of her, the butler had taken on a more parental concern when it came to her happiness.

"My lady, may I speak boldly?" Conrad shifted on his feet.

"Of course, Conrad."

"I don't trust Mr. Montgomery. After all, you found him in prison. I don't think—"

"Conrad," Gretta interrupted. "Mr. Montgomery is not who you think, and now that I know the real man behind his façade, I assure you, I will be safe in his presence." Just saying those words sent a strange warm feeling through her body. "He is going to help me find Charles."

Conrad's bushy eyebrows raised. "Your brother?"

"We have a lead to Charles' whereabouts and are going to follow up on it." Gretta reached out and grasped his hands. "He has a respectable job, so I shall be fine." Suddenly, she remembered Levi holding her in his arms while his luscious lips swept over hers, and she fought back the tingles threatening to disturb her. Why was she thinking of this now? She was determined never to let Levi into her life like that ever again.

"Very well, Lady Brinley. When can we expect your return?"

"Hopefully, by supper." She smiled. "I'm going to check on Uncle Reginald before I leave. If you see Mr. Montgomery, please let him know where I'm at."

"I will have Gilbert ready your coach."

She released Conrad's hands as he nodded. Gretta hurried to Uncle Reginald's room. She was too distraught last night to stop in to see him, and she wasn't going to make that mistake today. She must let him know her plans to find Charles and bring him to the manor. Hopefully that would cheer him up.

Gretta placed her hand on the doorknob and twisted just as the door swung open, pulling her into the room. Without being able to stop herself, she bumped into a strong muscular chest. She let go of the door and placed her hands on Levi's chest. Heat pulsed through her, so she quickly stepped away.

"Gretta," Levi said first. "I'm sorry, I didn't know you were coming in."

"It's my fault." She sucked in a quick breath as she gazed over him. He wasn't wearing the footman's clothing, but another one of Uncle Reginald's suits. Levi wore grey trousers and a white shirt with a matching gray vest. He looked as breathtaking as he did last night. "I wanted to visit Uncle Reginald before leaving."

"Gretta, we need to talk," he whispered, "concerning Uncle Reginald."

She quickly looked at the old man lying in the bed. He wasn't awake, it was too early.

"What is your concern?" Gretta asked.

"Uncle Reginald has been sleeping quite a bit. I stepped in last night to check on him before retiring to bed and his breathing was labored. I had to shake him a few times to get him to take some deeper breaths."

Gretta kept her focus on her uncle. He seemed to be resting just fine now. The couch in his room had been moved closer to the bed. A blanket was folded up and placed on a pillow. She swung her attention back to Levi.

"Did you sleep here last night?" she asked.

"Gretta, he is dying," Levi replied softly. "I stayed with him, hoping to keep him alive. When I heard him snoring softly, I fell asleep on the couch. Usually when people are dying, they sleep more. I haven't been able to wake him up this morning to take a drink."

Pain tightened in her chest and tears clouded her vision. She blinked multiple times then quickly wiped her cheeks. She knew the day was coming, but she hoped that it wouldn't be so soon.

"We need to find Charles," Gretta pleaded. "How long does Uncle Reginald have?"

Levi shook his head. "Only God knows."

Gretta hurried over to the bedside, grasped her uncle's hands and brought them to her lips, kissing them. More tears leaked from her eyes.

"Please, Uncle Reginald, hold on. We are bringing Charles home. I promise," she whispered.

"Gretta, we must hurry," Levi said. "I'll go out the back door."

"Levi," she said, wiping her face again. "Thank you for staying with him."

"It is what you assigned me to do for you." His gaze locked on hers. "But know this—I'll do *anything* you ask, Gretta." Levi turned and left the room.

Her mind was so conflicted. She must keep in mind that Levi lied and used her. She didn't want her heart to be deceived by his fake charm again.

Gretta's Gamble

Gretta gave Levi some time to move around to the front of the house, then she hurried outside. Gilbert opened the coach door and Levi helped her inside. The driver kept giving Levi an untrusting stare, and she wondered if her servant recognized Levi at all, especially since he was in the disguise he had worn last night.

"Gilbert, this is my cousin, Leviticus Montgomery," Gretta said. "You don't need to worry."

"Yes, Lady Brinley." Gilbert nodded.

"Gilbert, please take us to the waterfront district," Levi instructed as he stepped inside the coach.

Gilbert nodded politely and closed the door. The vehicle shook as he climbed up front, and minutes later, they were moving. Gretta looked out her window toward her manor. It was hard leaving Uncle Reginald knowing he was knocking on God's door. But right now, Charles needed to be her main focus.

Lord, please be with my uncle and not let him die yet.

CHAPTER THIRTEEN

During their journey, Levi kept mostly silent, only speaking when Gretta asked him a question. Small talk was not happening between them even if it was driving him insane. But he could see she kept their outing very proper between them.

They reached the waterfront, and the vehicle slowed slightly. Levi adjusted the fake mustache on his upper lip. It had become itchy, but he needed to keep with the disguise of being her cousin in case they ran into anyone she knew.

"Is it on straight?" Levi asked, looking at her.

She bit her bottom lip softly sending his heart racing again. Gretta carefully reached over and pressed it above his lip. It took every ounce of strength not to kiss her fingers. When her gaze met his, he wanted to pull her into his arms and beg for forgiveness. Gretta quickly broke the link between them before he gave into temptation.

"There, your mustache is much straighter now, Cousin Leviticus." She looked out the window again.

He grinned slightly, knowing she was still willing to play along with the charade. He moved his gaze out the window and noticed the sign above one of the shops. *Holt Lumber Company*. Hope grew inside Levi. This was one of his friend's lumber stores. Levi recalled Harrison Holt talking about his new shop in New York City, but Levi wasn't quite sure where it was. With Harrison's shop being along the waterfront, Levi prayed his friend might have seen Charles. It couldn't hurt to ask.

Levi knocked loudly on the wall of the coach and Gilbert slowed it down until it came to a complete stop.

"Why are we stopping already?" Gretta asked.

Gretta's Gamble

"My friend owns this place." He pointed to the store. "I'm hoping he is working at this location today. Harrison sees many people in this area, so there is a possibility that he has seen Charles."

The door opened and Gilbert stepped aside to let Levi exit. As he reached to assist Gretta down, the driver moved in front of him, not letting him take her hand. Grumbling under his breath, Levi stood back and didn't make a scene. After all, he was supposed to be her *cousin*. Now he wondered why he hadn't played the part of her beau or husband.

Many people wandered the area for being so early in the morning. The smell of the salty ocean drifted all around them.

Levi offered his arm, which thankfully, Gretta took, as he led the way to the front door of the lumber store. He opened it and allowed her to enter first.

The building smelled strongly of oak. A few men sat behind desks writing logs in journals. In the back corner sat a larger office. The familiar features of his friend Harrison came into view, and Levi sighed with relief. Now he prayed Harrison had seen Charles.

Harrison had a customer in his office, so Levi waited patiently. The large man talking to Harrison blocked his view from seeing Levi.

"May I help you, sir?" one of the other men close by asked.

"No, but thank you. I'm waiting for my friend, Mr. Holt." Levi motioned toward the office, not taking his gaze off Harrison.

Finally, Harrison moved toward the door and opened it, letting the customer leave first. Harrison glanced toward Levi, and then blinked as if not believing his eyes. He stepped closer to Levi, sweeping his stare over Gretta before moving it back to Levi. The man's eyebrows rose in recognition. The closer he came, his smile stretched wide.

"Well, if it isn't my friend, Levi Montgomery." Harrison laughed. "What do I owe the pleasure of your company?"

Levi held out his hand for Harrison to shake, and Harrison pulled him into a brotherly hug.

"I guess my disguise didn't fool you," Levi whispered as he touched his fake mustache.

"You forget, my friend, that I have been able to see through your disguises for years now." Harrison clapped a hand on Levi's shoulder. "Welcome to my new store." He looked at Gretta. "We aren't building you two a home, are we?"

Gretta's cheeks turned pink, and Levi barked out a loud laugh, feeling embarrassed, remembering the wager his childhood friends had made about getting married. He wanted to wipe Harrison's expression off his face since he looked as if he had won the best card game ever.

"My, aren't you being humorous today," Levi said. "But may I introduce you to Countess Brinley?"

"Brinley? I have heard that name before." Harrison took her hand and brought it to his lips to kiss her knuckles. "There was an English gent, about a year ago who used to play cards at Jones' Tavern. Any relation?"

Gretta smiled cordially. "If his name was Frederick, then he was my husband."

"Was?" Harrison looked again at Levi, as if he had something to do with this.

"Lady Brinley is a widow. I'm her cousin," Levi said a bit louder in case the others were listening.

Harrison's eyes widened, but seconds later, his expression changed to one of understanding. "I'm very sorry for your loss, Lady Brinley." Harrison nodded apologetically. "What brings you to my store?"

Gretta pulled out a small piece of canvas from her wrist purse. Levi leaned over to see what she had. It was a drawing of Charles. The man looked quite young, so Levi wondered how old the picture was.

"I'm looking for my brother." Gretta showed the picture to Harrison. "He would look a bit older. But he enjoys card games like my husband did. His hair is the same color as mine, just like his eyes."

Gretta's Gamble

"We believe he is in trouble," Levi added in a quieter voice. "He most likely has been hiding or in disguise. Have you seen anyone around the docks who could look like this man?"

Harrison's focus shifted between Gretta and the drawing, then shook his head. "Many people come and go in this area. Some board ships on the other end of the pier and I never see them again."

Gretta's shoulders drooped and she lowered her head in disappointment. Harrison handed the drawing back to her.

Harrison sighed, pushing his fingers through his dark brown hair. "How long has he been missing?"

"I haven't seen him in at least a year," Gretta replied. "I need to find him. Our uncle is dying, and I want Charles to see him before he passes."

"I'm very sorry, Lady Brinley," Harrison replied.

"The last someone had seen him was about four months ago. We lost sight of him." Levi looked around the shop. "I must say, my friend, you have done well for yourself."

"I couldn't have done this myself. I have many helpers. I have provided jobs for several homeless men." Harrison paused. "In fact, I have a few employees that might be able to help you. They know the docks and the people much better than I do." He put his hand on Gretta's arm. "Come with me."

They followed Harrison out to the back where workers were loading railroad ties in crates. There were at least ten men ranging in age from what looked to be twenty years to maybe forty years old.

"Men, may I have your attention," Harrison announced. Everyone stopped to listen. "This lovely lady is searching for someone. Please give her your attention as you might have seen this man around the waterfront."

While Gretta stepped forward to speak, Levi carefully studied each man. If someone was lying, he would be able to spot it in a heartbeat.

"His name is Charles Ramsay," Gretta began. "He has dark hair and is about six feet tall." She used her hand to show the height. "He is only two years older than me."

Out of all the men who were there, Levi noticed that one kept his head down. He shifted nervously as if he were looking for a way out of the area. The man had a thick beard and wore ragged clothing. He leaned heavily on a crutch.

"It is very important that we find him," Gretta continued. "Please, if anyone has seen him, I need to know."

The men shook their heads then returned to work. Harrison put his hand on Gretta again, frowning in disappointment. Levi wished his friend would stop touching her. That was *his* job, if she would ever allow him to do so again.

"I'm sorry," Harrison said. "I have some other workers who will come in this afternoon when the shift changes. If you want to return around three o'clock, we can do this again."

"Thank you, Mr. Holt. I appreciate your kindness." Gretta smiled, allowing Harrison to move his arm around her shoulder as they walked back toward the building.

Levi fisted his hands by his sides. He didn't understand the jealousy filling him, and he wished he wouldn't feel so possessive. But he saw Gretta first. Harrison had no right to charm her.

Before following the other two, he took one more look over his shoulder toward Harrison's workers. The cowering man in the back quickly turned and tried to limp away. Levi's gut feeling was that this man knew something. He couldn't let the man leave.

* * * *

Gretta stared at Levi's friend. Harrison Holt wasn't bad on the eyes. His height, broad shoulders, and heart-warming brown eyes would make any woman turn their head. He also had the talent of charm, much like his friend, Levi. Was there a school in America that men attended who taught them this trait? Frederick, an Englishman born and raised, had certainly never obtained that talent.

She peeked behind her to see if Levi was following, but he wasn't. She was sure that the Pinkerton agent in him wanted to talk to the men separately. Although it was despairing that none of Mr. Holt's workers recognized Charles, she couldn't give up hope.

When she turned her attention back to Mr. Holt, he was looking at her. Gone was his concerned expression, and in its place was a look of interest.

"I hope you don't mind me asking," he said. "But how did you and Levi meet?"

She tried not to let the man see her irritation in Levi, especially how they met. "I'm one of his cases."

Mr. Holt's eyes widened. "How can that be? Pinkerton agents only search for criminals."

She shrugged. "Well, because he thinks my brother is a thief, I'm obviously connected to the case."

Mr. Holt narrowed his eyes. "Am I to assume that you don't think your brother is a thief?"

"Correct, sir."

Slowly, the man's smile returned. "So, you are accompanying Levi to prove him wrong?"

Gretta wasn't prepared for his question, and a laugh escaped her throat. "I suppose you can put it that way."

Mr. Holt grinned wider. "How fun is that? I'm sure your resistance makes Levi want to prove his point that much more."

"Indeed. Your friend can be persistent at times." But she wasn't going to comment about how endearing Levi could be as well. How could a man set on deceiving her just to find Charles, have such a kind heart? She would never forget the way Levi went out of his way to care for Uncle Reginald... and to think Levi spent the night in her uncle's room just to make sure he was breathing. How could she keep her heart from softening toward him now?

He patted her hand still hooked over his arm. "And from the little I know about you, just in the time we have talked, I'm happy to know you are standing by your beliefs. Whether Levi will admit it or not, he needs someone like you in his life."

Gretta's heartbeat skipped erratically. Why did Mr. Holt tell her something as bold as *that*? Perhaps men in America said what was on their mind whether it was improper or not.

She lifted her chin, stubbornly. "Well, I'm only in his life until we find Charles. Then I hope Levi leaves as quickly as he came."

They stepped in to the main building, but Levi still wasn't anywhere around. Gretta didn't know if she needed to be worried or not. After all, she saw the frustration in his eyes when Gilbert helped her from the coach instead of Levi, and the jealousy in his expression when Mr. Holt gave her so much attention. She suspected Levi would stay nearby, so why wasn't he?

"Lady Brinley?" Mr. Holt asked. "Would you like a tour of my new store?"

Levi's friend was sweet, and under any other circumstances, she would have accepted, but now was not the time. "I appreciate your offer, but I must see what Levi is up to. I suspect he is asking your workers questions, and since our visit is about my brother, I feel that I should be with him."

A knowing grin relaxed on Mr. Holt's handsome face, bringing a sparkle to his brown eyes. "Yes, that is probably a good idea."

He turned them back toward the door, but she stopped him. "Mr. Holt, I don't want to keep you from your job any longer. I can find my way back to the others."

"Are you sure?"

She nodded. "Thank you for your hospitality. It was very nice meeting you."

Mr. Holt lifted her hand from his arm and to his mouth, brushing a feathery kiss on her knuckles. "And it was a pleasure to meet such a lovely lady like you, Lady Brinley."

Feeling his warm breath on her hand didn't stir butterflies in her stomach like when Levi had done that. Inwardly, she cursed the man's ability to make her weak in the knees. Of course, it didn't help that her lips still burned with tingles every time she thought about the way he kissed her.

Gretta's Gamble

Gretta quickened her pace, retracing her steps back toward Levi. This insanity must end soon. She couldn't think about him that way and at the same time, want him out of her life for good.

As she approached the group of workers, she couldn't see Levi. She moved toward the back and noticed him in an alley between two buildings. Levi stood in front of a man leaning against a crutch. Levi's hand gripped the man's upper arm as if he was keeping him still. The expression on the agent's face let her know he wasn't very happy.

Curiosity moved her feet faster, but then irritation grew inside her to think that Levi was so brutally mean with this disabled man, when she saw firsthand how gentle he had been to Uncle Reginald. She must remember not to spout her anger in front of Mr. Holt's worker, but to wait until she and Levi were in the coach and let him know how she felt about the harsh way he handled the crippled man.

The worker's bushy beard and straggly hair were a dark brown, but there was so much dirt on him, she wondered what the man's true hair color was. He wore round spectacles, and yet the glass didn't look dirty like the rest of him. In fact, as she came closer, she wondered if there was any glass in them at all.

"Why are you doing this to her?" Levi snapped, but his voice was low as though he didn't want anyone else to hear their conversation.

"Please, sir," the man's voice cracked. "I don't know what you're talking about."

Levi shook the man's arm once. "You think I'm a fool? I've been an investigator for several years. I know how to spot a man in disguise."

The man shook his head. "I'm not who you accuse me of being."

"Really? How many men in New York do you know who has an English accent? No matter how much you have disguised yourself, you have the same similarities as Charles Ramsay."

Gretta gasped and stopped short, making both men turn their head to look at her. Her focus was on the crippled man, studying him closer now. Levi was correct. If the worker washed and cut his hair and beard, he would resemble her brother perfectly. And now she could see that his spectacles didn't have any glass in them.

"Charles?" she whispered tightly, stepping closer to him. The man quickly ducked his head, keeping from looking directly at her.

"No, ma'am. I'm not the man you seek."

The fierce beating of her heart made her breathless. Her head pounded with uncertainty, and yet... she *knew* this was her brother.

"Charles, please look at me." She touched his shoulder. "Tell me why you are in hiding."

The man blinked rapidly but she still detected tears in his eyes. Happiness burst inside her as she teared up. "Oh, Charles." Her voice broke. "I have finally found you."

Slowly, the man looked up and met her stare. The brown eyes looking at her were indeed her brother's. Her strength from being strong all this time crumbled and she fell against him, wrapping her arms around his thin shoulders. He had lost weight, but she didn't care. At least he was with her now and she would do anything to protect him.

Charles' body shook as if he was silently crying. Gradually, he slid an arm around her waist, pulling her closer. That only made her cry harder.

"Oh, Etta," Charles mumbled, calling her the nickname he'd given her when they were young. "Forgive me for worrying you so. I'm in hiding to keep safe, and to keep you safe, as well."

She pulled back and stared into his eyes. Touching his cheek, her stomach twisted. "You are in danger, aren't you?"

He nodded.

"Why?"

"I don't know." He shrugged. "I haven't done anything wrong, but in the last year, someone has been following me and causing accidents to injure me." He tapped his right leg. "I was shot at just two months ago."

Panic filled her, and she swung her head toward Levi. She was surprised that he wasn't scowling. In fact, he looked concerned. "Levi, will you help him?"

"Charles, I want to know if you stole Mrs. Kensington's heart-shaped ruby necklace. That is my assignment and why I've been trying to find you."

"I did not, sir, but I know who did."

Gretta's heartbeat quickened. Could this case be solved so soon? She prayed Charles had all the answers. Then maybe Levi would dismiss the idea of putting her brother in jail.

"Who was it?" Levi asked, stepping closer to Gretta as he stared at Charles. "Please, man. You must tell us. The thief needs to be caught."

Charles nodded as his gaze jumped back and forth between her and Levi. She didn't exactly like the way her brother's wary-eyed expression made her feel.

"Charles? Please, tell us."

Her brother swallowed hard as his focus rested on her. Sighing heavily, he touched her arm. "The true thief was… Frederick."

CHAPTER FOURTEEN

Gretta's head rang with the words her brother had said, but nothing was registering. She couldn't have heard him correctly. Why would Frederick steal the necklace? Then again, Levi had mentioned that this case was ongoing for about a year.

She lifted a shaky hand to her throat and narrowed her eyes to Charles. "Frederick stole the heart-shaped ruby necklace? The same one he gave me for our anniversary?"

Charles nodded. "I had attended the party given by Mr. and Mrs. Kensington." He looked at Levi. "Which is probably why people thought I had stolen it, but I didn't."

"What really happened that night?" Gretta asked.

Charles glanced down the alley toward the other men. "I can't talk here. I don't know who to trust."

"Trust us." She took her brother's hand. "Come back to the manor with us. We will protect you."

"If someone is truly after you," Levi added, "then being with a Pinkerton agent is safer than out in the open."

"No," Charles said sharply. "The reason I went into hiding is because someone wants me dead. If I come with you to the manor, I'm putting my sister in danger."

She inhaled slowly and released it quickly. "Charles, Uncle Reginald is dying. If you don't get to say goodbye before he dies, you'll never forgive yourself."

Charles' frown deepened. "How much longer does he have?"

Gretta looked at Levi who was watching her. The tightness in her chest increased. "Not long, according to Levi."

"Your sister is correct. Lord Reynolds doesn't have much time at all. In fact, he may be gone by the time we get back."

Gretta's Gamble

"No, he won't be dead." Gretta squared her shoulders as she fought back a new batch of tears. "Before we left this morning, I told him to hang on because I was bringing Charles back." She turned back to her brother. "Please, Charles."

He nodded. "I need to tell Mr. Holt."

"Let me," Levi said. "Gretta, you take your brother to the coach, and I'll tell my friend."

She touched Levi's hand. "Let Mr. Holt know not to say anything to the others. If my brother's life is in danger, we don't need anyone knowing I have found him."

"Agreed."

"Gretta, go get in the coach and I'll come afterward." Charles motioned a hand toward the main building. "If the others see us walking together, they will know."

"Quite right, Charles." She smiled. "But don't be long." She switched her focus to Levi. "And the same thing with you. Please, hurry."

The men agreed, so she walked beside Levi back toward the store. As he entered the building, she continued until she reached the vehicle. Gilbert jumped down and opened the door.

"Gilbert," she said softly, "we found my brother."

The driver's eyes widened, and his mouth hung open. "So, when you see a man in a beard walking with a crutch coming toward us, let him inside quickly."

"Yes, my lady."

After he helped her into the coach, he closed the door. Although relief filled her, so did worry. They found Charles, but he must say his goodbyes to their uncle. And then, once that was finished, they needed to discover why someone wanted to harm Charles. She prayed Levi would help her one last time.

She heard voices outside, and seconds later, the door opened, and Levi climbed inside. He sat across from her but met her gaze.

"Are you all right?" he asked.

"I will be once we get back to the manor."

He leaned forward and took her hand in a gentle hold. His thumb stroked her knuckles. "Gretta, I won't let anything happen to your brother."

"Do you believe he is innocent then?"

"I do."

"How do you know?"

Levi smiled. "Because men who are guilty would have tried to run when we showed up. Guilty men wouldn't have made themselves look conspicuous. They would have gone about their work as if nothing was wrong. Charles didn't do that, which is why I became suspicious. And watching your brother's actions, I do believe he is in danger."

Her eyes filled with tears again. She had been trying to stay brave in his presence, but sometimes she just wanted him to hold her and let her know everything would be all right. Yet she couldn't.... she wouldn't.

He cupped the side of her face. "You don't have to do this alone. I will be there—if you allow me to help."

She swallowed hard and nodded. "Thank you, Levi. You are better prepared for this type of situation than I am, so yes, I would like your help."

"You can always count on me, Gretta."

She fought the ugly cry that was filling her, but she didn't want him to see her weak like this. However, her heart softened that much more for the man she didn't want to forgive.

"Levi? Why are you doing this?"

He drew the pad of his thumb across her cheek. "Doing what, my lovely Gretta?"

"Why are you still trying to charm me when you know how I feel about you?"

He chuckled softly. "Because I hurt you, and I'll be forever sorry. But I also believe that your hurt has made you *think* you hate me, but I know better."

She arched an eyebrow. "You know better?"

He nodded. "I will always remember how you felt in my arms with your mouth against mine in a passionate kiss. A woman who kisses like you do can't hate the man she shared so much with that quickly."

Her breathing grew ragged. Why couldn't she control the flutters inside her when he was like this?

His gaze dropped to her mouth, and her throat turned dry. She couldn't let this tender moment turn into one of lonely desire. She must stay strong… but he made it so hard.

Thankfully, she heard voices outside the coach, which made Levi pull away. She also leaned against her seat, relieved that something stopped her from going with her first instincts.

The vehicle door opened, and Charles climbed inside and sat by Gretta. He wrapped both arms around her, giving her a big bear hug. She didn't care how filthy or smelly he was, she was just happy he was still alive and back in her life.

"I'm sorry for worrying you so, Etta," he whispered. "I promise never to do that to you again."

She pulled back and wiped the tears running down her cheeks. "And I shall hold you to that promise."

Charles looked at Levi. "I'm ready to go home now."

Gretta sighed. So was she.

* * * *

Levi paced the floor in the sitting room, waiting for Charles to make an appearance. Both brother and sister bathed and changed clothes as soon as they arrived back at the manor. Then, their plans were to spend some time with their uncle. Levi had already checked on the dying man, and although he was still alive, Levi doubted the man would be coherent enough to talk much. Lord Reynolds wouldn't make it through the night, Levi was certain of it.

But the wait tried his patience. He wanted answers about the stolen necklace. Why would so many reports mention Charles Ramsay as the thief instead of mentioning Frederick Brinley? Levi didn't doubt the gambling man had stolen the heirloom and given it to Gretta, but Levi couldn't figure out why the man hadn't tried to sell it and use the money for his gambling habit?

It frustrated him to think that finding Charles only created more questions. Would this case ever get solved? At least he would be able to return the necklace to Mrs. Kensington. But when would he figure out what really happened and why?

He paused in his pacing and glanced toward the door, listening for voices. But he didn't hear any.

Grumbling under his breath, he walked to the window and peered outside toward Gretta's flower garden. A smile pulled on his scowl and made his heart light. How had he allowed her to get under his skin? It wasn't that he just desired her anymore, but he longed to be with her. He wanted to help her and her uncle, and yes, even her wayward brother. And more than anything, he wanted her forgiveness for breaking her heart and to see her appreciative twinkle in her pretty eyes.

He wished she would look at him again as though he was the most important person in her life. He wanted her to desire him as he still yearned for her.

He groaned and leaned his forehead against the windowpane. Indeed, he was a fallen man. Somehow, her sweetness had lured him to her side, and now he didn't want to leave.

His mind returned to the card game he had with his six friends, and especially the wager they had. The first one to fall in love and marry would have to give up something they cherished more than anything. He had wagered his grandmother's pearl necklace—the necklace he had promised his grandmother to give to his bride. Yet if he married, he wouldn't have the pearl necklace at all.

Somehow, it wasn't important any longer. Somehow… Gretta had become more important than the necklace.

His chest tightened with an unknown emotion. Could it be love? Four months ago, he had thought he was in love with Alexa Moore. Now he realized that hadn't been love at all because he had never felt so strongly about her as he felt for Gretta. He couldn't believe he was going to be the first out of his friends to break the wager, but at this moment, he didn't care.

Gretta's Gamble

Voices echoed down the hall, and he swung away from the window and hurried toward the door. When he saw Gretta, his heartbeat quickened. Heavens, she was so very lovely wearing a lavender gown with black trim. Her hair flowed long over her shoulders, just as he liked, and she only had the sides of her hair pulled back away from her face with combs. Her eyes were red and puffy as she had been crying. Even Charles appeared as if he had been crying too. Levi could now see the resemblance between brother and sister, now that Charles had cleaned himself up and shaved off the beard.

"How... is your uncle?" Levi asked hesitantly, thinking he already knew the answer because of their tears.

Gretta wiped her eyes and tried to smile. "He was able to chat briefly with Charles, but he fell back asleep." She struggled with a deep breath. "I fear he may not make it through the night."

"At least I got to say goodbye." Charles' voice cracked, so he cleared his throat.

Gretta took her brother's hand and squeezed. "Thankfully, we found you just in time."

"Indeed." Charles kissed his sister's hand and released it before walking to the tray of brandy. "Montgomery? Would you like a drink as well?"

"Thank you, but no." Levi stepped aside and let Gretta walk to the sofa to sit before he joined her. He was relieved that she didn't ask him to find a different chair.

Charles tossed down a healthy swallow of brandy before moving to the single cushioned chair in the room and sat. He exhaled a ragged breath before taking another drink.

"I hope you are ready to tell us what happened that night at Mrs. Kensington's party," Levi said.

Charles nodded. "I am." He looked at Gretta. "As I had mentioned earlier, I was in attendance at Mrs. Kensington's party, just as Frederick. It surprised me that he hadn't brought you with him, but then I remembered that he never took you to functions like that."

"I hope you don't mind me asking," Levi began, "what do you mean by *functions like that*? Didn't Mrs. Kensington have regular parties like other wealthy women in New York City?"

Chuckling, Charles shook his head. "Etta, forgive me if what I say burns your ears or offends your sensibilities, but it's important you know about the party."

"I shall be fine, I assure you." She straightened in her seat.

"Mrs. Kensington's parties tend to run a little more risqué than some of the parties in New York. Many of the people who came knew they would be finding another partner to um… sneak off in an attempt to get to know them better, if you know what I mean."

Inwardly, Levi groaned, wishing Charles wouldn't be so blunt in front of Gretta. Her face reddened, but she acted as though she wasn't offended, even though Levi knew differently.

"Anyway," Charles continued. "I went to the party to meet up with Mrs. Kensington's youngest daughter. In fact, Miss Kensington invited me to the event. Not only that, but I knew there would be a challenging card game, and of course, I wanted to join." Charles took another drink of his brandy, finishing what was left in the glass. "Later in the evening, after I left the poker table, I noticed Frederick coming down the grand staircase alone. I figured he had just been—"

"Yes, Charles," Levi quickly interrupted. "We get the picture." His heart was breaking for Gretta who had to listen to the story about her husband who obviously didn't love her and had to find entertainment elsewhere.

"Of course, Montgomery." He frowned, looking at Gretta again. "I'm sorry you have to hear this about Frederick."

She flipped her hand in the air. "It's not the first time I have heard about his extra marital affairs, and I'm sure I've heard worse than what you are going to tell us."

Charles cleared his throat. "But Frederick didn't see me because he was so busy hurrying down the stairs as he stuffed something inside his long-tailed coat. I watched him rush out of the manor, and he never returned. However, I did meet up with Miss Kensington and was kept busy the rest of the night. Very early the next morning, she walked me to my horse and kissed me goodbye."

Levi leaned forward, resting his forearms on his knees. "So, Miss Kensington could be your alibi?"

Charles rolled his eyes. "I doubt she will, because then the truth would come out and her parents might force us to marry, but I assure you, I was not her first."

"Charles?" Gretta asked. "What day was this party?"

His frown deepened. "One week before your anniversary. When you showed me what Frederick gave you, I knew your husband couldn't afford such an expensive piece of jewelry. I also remember seeing Mrs. Kensington wear that same necklace a few days before the party."

"Why…" Gretta's voice shook. "Why didn't you tell me?"

"I couldn't, Etta. I worried that I was wrong about Frederick, but I didn't want you to hurt any more. I knew you were not happy in your marriage, and seeing how happy the necklace made you, I couldn't break your heart."

She laughed forcefully. "The only reason the necklace made me happy was because my husband actually remembered our anniversary, and because the only other piece of jewelry he gave me was my wedding band."

Levi wished Frederick was still alive, only because he wanted the enjoyment of plowing his fist into the man's face for making Gretta feel so worthless. Levi would never do that to her.

He just prayed she gave him a second chance to prove that.

CHAPTER FIFTEEN

Gretta couldn't hold it together any longer. Her nerves had been worn, as well as the taxing journey to find Charles. She needed sleep—and a good cry. Probably not in that order, though.

After excusing herself, explaining that she was tired, she left Levi and her brother to talk over other questions that arose during their conversation. She wasn't sure which exhausted her the most—the journey to find her brother or reliving her insecurities when she had been married to Frederick. She hadn't wanted Levi to see that the topic had bothered her, only because she wished she had never married Frederick and wasted that time in her life. She had learned one thing during that terrible time—that servants were people too, and they were as lonely for a friend as she had been.

She entered her room and waited as her maid undressed her before she dismissed the servant. Gretta sat at her vanity table and brushed her hair, staring at the pathetic woman in the mirror. When would she ever forget her marriage? She wanted to feel like a real woman and have the experiences that she had missed out on.

But she had felt somewhat valuable before discovering Levi's true identity. Dare she believe him when he told her that he hadn't lied about desiring her? If only she could trust him, then she might welcome him back into her life—even though he had never really left. And just thinking of the day he finally closed the case and left, made her stomach churn with knots.

In such a short amount of time, he had become important in her life. He was the man she felt safe with, the one who comforted her when she was upset. She had looked forward to seeing him each day and missed him after they parted ways at night. She wouldn't be able to be happy if he left her again. She loved him, and she needed to tell him—tonight—if just for her peace of mind.

She prayed he returned her feelings, but if not, at least she tried. Never again did she want to be stuck in a loveless marriage. If they were meant to be together, they would find a way. She must accept God's plan for her.

Decision made, she tossed her brush on the table, stood, and retrieved her wrapper. As she headed for the door, she shrugged into it.

Leaving her quarters, she tiptoed down the hall, hoping nobody heard her sneaking out. Especially not her brother. Although she was thrilled he was back, she knew he would try to protect her and stop her from meeting a man in private. She couldn't let him do that tonight of all nights.

Gretta took soft steps toward Levi's room. She paused in front of the door, listening for any sounds coming from within. She didn't detect any.

She rested her hand on the doorknob and slowly turned it until it opened. She peeked inside the small room, but the bed was empty. A small lamp was dimly lit, but Levi was nowhere in sight.

Disappointment washed through her, and she backed out, closing the door. As she headed down the hall, her mind spun with ideas of where he could be. Perhaps he was in Uncle Reginald's room again, just as he had been last night.

With renewed enthusiasm, she hurried down the stairs toward her uncle's room. Not wanting to disturb him, she quietly opened the door and walked inside. Once again, she was disappointed when she didn't see Levi.

She stepped closer to the bed to check on her uncle. Thankfully, he was still breathing, but it was laborious. It saddened her to think there was nothing anyone could do to make him well. He had lived a good life and made many people happy. Sadly, he never married or had children. He always thought of her and Charles as his own children, and after her father died, she thought of Uncle Reginald as her parent.

Gretta leaned over and softly kissed his forehead. "Good night, my sweet uncle," she whispered. "I'm so grateful to you for everything you have done for me, but I must tell you that… I'm in love with Levi Montgomery. I know you don't like him very well, but I believe he is a good man and I want him in my life. I'm going to tell him tonight, so please understand." She swept her fingers over his brow. She knew he wouldn't answer her, but she felt like he approved of her decision. "I have known you were dying for some time, but I never wanted to fully admit it. But I will accept God's will. When you make it to Heaven, tell my parents I miss them so much, but they shouldn't worry about me and Charles. Levi will protect us."

Gretta watched the rise and fall of his chest as the pace slowed considerably… until it stopped moving. She touched the side of his neck to feel for a pulse—which was what she saw Levi do once—but she couldn't feel one. She placed her fingers under his nose to feel his breath, but once again, it wasn't detected.

Tears filled her eyes, and she was blessed to have been with her uncle the moment he left this world. "Goodbye, Uncle Reginald. Fly high with the angels."

She knelt by his bed and rested her head against his frail shoulder as the tears poured down her face. Yet, she was at peace because she knew her uncle was no longer in pain. She would miss him, but he was much happier now in Heaven.

Loneliness crept over her, and she realized she didn't want to spend this mourning time alone. She should run to get her brother, yet he wasn't the man she wanted to share this moment with. She wanted Levi.

She jumped to her feet and dashed out the door, closing it behind her. Although she tried to be quiet so as not to wake anyone in the household, she hurried out of the manor, heading toward the stable. That was the only other place Levi could be tonight. The first day she brought him home, he had told her how much he loved horses.

Gretta's Gamble

Warm air touched her face, and she was happy the night wasn't colder, but it didn't keep her from running toward the stable anyway. The moon's sliver of light didn't brighten the way for her, but this way was better so that nobody would see where she was heading in her nightclothes.

As she neared the structure, she noticed a light inside. Her heart leapt with relief, yet she was also very nervous. This was the first time of telling a man she had fallen in love with him. Thankfully, she could never say that to Frederick.

The stable door didn't squeak when she opened it, and she was able to step inside without him hearing. He stood by her favorite horse, running a brush over the animal's mane. She stood still for several seconds, enjoying the sound as he hummed a calming tune. She loved his baritone voice. He could sing to her any time.

As much as she wanted to stare at him longer, she needed him now. She needed his arms around her in a comforting hug.

Two steps toward him, she stepped on dry straw, and it cracked. His humming stopped and he spun toward her. When he recognized her, his eyes widened, and his mouth hung open. But then he must have noticed her tears, and a saddened frown took over his expression.

He threw the animal's brush on the table while still holding her gaze and came toward her. She reached out her arms, and when their bodies met, he took her into a comforting embrace.

"He's... gone," she said brokenly.

"I'm so sorry, Gretta." Levi swept his lips across her forehead.

"I... didn't want to be alone right now."

"No, you shouldn't have to be. I'm here. I'll always be here for you."

Closing her eyes, she pressed against him, burying her face next to his muscular chest as she cried out her sorrow. Yet being with Levi now didn't make her sad at all. Relief and happiness were the words to explain her emotions.

He held her tightly for a little while longer before she was able to stop crying. She didn't want to move. She enjoyed this relaxed sensation too much. But she wanted to express her feelings to him. She had come too far to back down now.

Gretta tilted her head back and looked into his watery eyes. It delighted her to know he was sharing her grief.

"Thank you, Levi."

His smile was soothing. "For what?"

"For being with me."

His hand lifted to her hair and stroked her locks. "There is no other place I would rather be during this time of mourning."

She shook her head. "No, I mean for being with me this whole time. I don't know what I would have done without you."

His face relaxed. "Gretta, you were more than just my *next case*. I came to care for you more than I was prepared for. That was why I couldn't leave you. It had nothing to do with your brother, either."

Her heart softened and she smiled. "Levi Montgomery, you are the first man that I've met who has stirred my emotions so drastically in just a short amount of time. There were times I wanted to strangle you and times I wanted to do nothing but kiss you endlessly."

His grin widened. "Oh, really?"

She chuckled softly. "Indeed. You can be irritatingly convincing."

He shrugged. "I was determined to make you like me."

The rhythm of her heartbeat quickened as she slowly shook her head. "But that's the point, Levi. I don't like you."

He arched an eyebrow. "You don't? Well, you don't show it very well then."

"It's because... I'm in *love* with you, Levi Montgomery."

Humor disappeared from his expression as his eyes widened. "You truly love me?"

She nodded. "I fought my feelings after I discovered you were a Pinkerton agent, but because of the way you showed your kindness, I knew I couldn't be mad at you for long." She caressed the side of his face briefly before running her fingers through his hair. "You are an amazing man, and you will always have a place in my heart... and in my life."

His beautiful blue-eyed gaze softened. "Oh, Gretta. I, too, have been fighting my feelings for you. I didn't want to give my heart away, only because the last time I tried, I was rejected. But I realized today that the way I feel for you is much stronger than the way I felt for the other woman. I know now, beyond a shadow of a doubt, that I'm madly in love with you."

Happiness burst in her chest. She threw her arms around his neck and met his kiss. His arms tightened around her as his palms slid over her back, pulling her closer. He kissed her so passionately, but it was also so very urgent as if he couldn't get enough. There was an intensity inside her as well, and she knew that kissing him in the stable was not that romantic. Dare she ask if he wanted to take it back to the manor?

She broke the kiss, even if she continued to leave feathery kisses along his jaw and down his neck.

"Levi," she muttered in between kisses, "would you think it bold of me if I suggest we continue this inside the manor? Maybe even my chambers—"

Before she could finish her thoughts, he groaned as his mouth covered hers again, and kissed her hungrily. He shifted her in his arms until he lifted her, carrying her toward the door. He broke the kiss a few times to see where he was walking.

She moved her lips down to his neck again. She loved hearing his gasps of delight, and she knew she was moaning with pleasure as well.

Every once in a while, his mouth moved to hers, but his determined steps took them toward the manor.

"Gretta," he said in a voice that sounded too deep to be coming from him.

"Yes?"

"I hope you don't think that I've picked an inappropriate time to ask this question, but..." He stopped and looked into her eyes. "Will you marry me?"

A giddy laugh sprang from her throat, and she nodded. "Oh, Levi. I will feel like the luckiest woman alive to be your wife."

"No, my love. The luck will be mine as well."

"I love you," she whispered, feeling as though she wanted to cry again.

"I love you more." He winked.

They reached the side door, and he stopped again, releasing her legs slowly until she was able to stand in front of him. He caressed her cheek and gazed into her eyes.

"What do you think your brother will think about us getting married?"

She snorted a laugh. "I don't think he will like it, but he will have to adjust because I'm not letting you out of my life, ever."

This time when Levi kissed her, it was softer and slower. She clung to his shirt, loving the way her heart burst with happiness.

He withdrew and opened the door for her. She entered, and then turned to take his hand. After the door closed behind them, they walked quietly toward the grand stairs.

Although she figured her staff was asleep, she didn't feel right. Something in the air warned her that she and Levi were not alone. She tried shrugging off the odd sensation making goosebumps rise on her skin… until she heard the floor creak.

Levi's steps stalled, as did hers. The corridor wasn't lit, which created shadows everywhere. The only light came from upstairs, and only a certain part of the hall was noticeable.

The floorboard creaked again, and a shadow moved toward them, coming into the small section of light. She held her breath… And then she saw the man pointing a pistol at her.

Her heart dropped and pain exploded in her head. No, it couldn't be. Why would she see *him* in her home?

She swallowed, trying to moisten her suddenly dry throat. "Frederick?"

Gretta's Gamble

CHAPTER SIXTEEN

Out of all the times for Levi to leave his pistol in his room, why did it have to be now? The dim lighting showed Gretta's face turning pale, and immediately, Levi wanted to protect her any way possible. Indeed, he needed his pistol.

The intruder who stood before them looked frazzled as if he carried a heavy burden on his own shoulders. But what scared Levi more was that the man looked determined.

He quickly pushed Gretta behind him, facing the intruder head-on. Flashbacks of him accidentally shooting Alexa haunted his memories. He never wanted anyone he loved to be harmed needlessly.

"Frederick?" Gretta asked again in a shaky voice. "You must be a ghost, because you shouldn't be here."

The man snorted out a laugh and motioned for them to move toward the grand staircase. "Gretta, I don't want to hurt you as long as you give me the ruby necklace."

"Who are you?" Levi growled.

"So, Gretta… I see you didn't waste any time replacing your deceased worthless husband." The man chuckled again. "Mr. Montgomery, I presume? I finally have the Pinkerton agent and the thorn in my side together in one place."

"You are not Frederick," Gretta snapped. "He would never speak to me in a condescending tone."

"There is so much you don't know about your dearly departed." The man snickered. "Frederick lied to you for such a long time. I felt bad for you because you clearly picked the wrong brother to love."

"Stop talking in riddles," she said angrily. "Tell me who you are and why you look like Frederick?"

He grinned. "I'm Richard Brinley—your deceased husband's brother. I was born five minutes earlier."

Levi gasped. "Twins?"

"Frederick never mentioned you," Gretta replied.

"Of course not. I've been disowned by the family for ten years now. My father thought I had poor judgment and lived a reckless life, unlike a *true* Englishman. The only one who cared about me was Frederick, the fool." He circled behind them as they climbed the stairs. "Now, take me to that necklace and a few other things I stashed here before my brother died, and then I'll be out of your way."

Levi didn't want to cause any sudden movements to irritate this man. He pressed on Gretta's back to have her ascend the stairs ahead of him. Thankfully, she took each step slowly.

"You couldn't have possibly kept items in the manor, especially if Frederick knew about it. Have you forgotten about his nasty habit of gambling?"

Richard's scowl darkened. "I swear, if my brother used any of those items, I'll—"

"You will do nothing," Levi said sharply. "Gretta didn't know about any of them, and since your brother was at fault and he is not here, you need to be the bigger man and move on."

Richard chuckled. "We shall see. But right now, I want my ruby necklace."

"I think you mean Mrs. Kensington's ruby necklace."

"It's not hers any longer." Richard motioned with his pistol toward the stairs. "You are walking too slow. Go faster."

"For your information," Gretta said, keeping her eyes forward as she walked, "I had to sell many things to pay off Frederick's debts after he died."

"Yes, sadly gambling ruins lives," Richard replied.

"And so does being a thief," Levi added.

"Not when you are a good thief. Thankfully, I had a scapegoat, so nobody knew it was me."

Gretta's Gamble

They reached the top of the stairs, and Gretta stopped, turning toward Richard. "You were using my brother, weren't you?"

Richard grinned boastfully. "Congratulations, Lady Brinley. You aren't as naïve as your brother told everyone you were."

"And let me guess," Levi interrupted. "You were also the one trying to kill him, which is why he went into hiding."

"I must say, Gretta. You picked a smart man this time, unlike the idiot you married."

Gretta fisted her hands. "Charles did nothing to you, so why involve him?"

"Your brother knew about me. Charles saw me coming down Mrs. Kensington's stairs and I was stuffing it in my overcoat. Of course, he thought I was Frederick. But those who knew I was going around town portraying your husband never said anything to you. They thought they could try and clear Frederick's name. But *that fool* shot the wrong brother."

Gretta's mouth dropped open in shock. "What are you saying?"

Levi shook his head. "Gretta, you can't believe this man. I talked to Charles and he hasn't killed anyone."

"I'm not talking about Charles."

"Then who?" she asked as her voice lifted.

"Your butler, Conrad."

Gretta gasped. "Conrad?"

"Keep walking," Richard said.

Gretta turned and continued walking toward her quarters. It irritated Levi that Richard wasn't making any sense. Levi just hoped she wasn't believing this man.

Levi shook his head. "You're trying to confuse us. If Conrad knew about you taking on your twin's identity, he would have told Gretta."

"No," she whispered brokenly. "Since I married Frederick, Conrad could see my misery and tried to protect me. He kept many things from me when it came to my husband's secret lifestyle."

They reached Gretta's bedchamber and stopped. Her door was already open. Levi suspected Richard had been trying to find the necklace already. The man motioned for them to step inside.

"I hid my other jewels under a loose floorboard underneath the bed. So be a good chap, Montgomery, and push the bed over, please," Richard ordered. "And Gretta, bring me the heart-shaped necklace."

Gretta peered at Levi, looking as helpless as he felt. He needed to do something, and do it quickly, or the thief would be gone again. Without a weapon, Levi wasn't sure how he could gain control over this situation.

He gave Gretta a nod then he walked to her bed. As he placed his hand on the bedpost of Gretta's canopy bed, the post wiggled. His gaze rose to the top of the canopy. She didn't have the curtain attached to it. The corners were just freestanding poles.

He glanced over his shoulder toward Richard. The man watched Gretta as she rummaged through the closet. She took down a jewelry box from the top shelf and turned to face Richard. While nobody was looking Levi's way, he wiggled the post a little more. This would slide out very easily, and soon his mind opened, giving him a way to take control—and have a weapon to use at the same time.

Just as he yanked on the bedpost, removing it from the frame, Gretta threw the jewelry box toward Richard's hand that held the gun. With the bedpost in his hands, he swung it toward Richard. The post whacked against Richard's back, and the man let out a painful grunt as the gun dropped to the ground.

Gretta backed into the closet to get out of the way while Levi swung the post again, hitting Richard over the head. The man crumbled to the floor. Levi dropped the post and retrieved the gun.

He pointed the pistol toward Richard and tsked. "You made a terrible mistake in coming, but I'm glad you still have poor judgment just as you did when your family disowned you."

Gretta's Gamble

Someone in the hallway screamed Gretta's name. She hurried out of the closet, stopping beside Levi as she looked toward the still open door of her room.

"We are in here, Charles."

Rushed footsteps hurried into the room and Gretta rushed into her brother's arms. Conrad was only a few steps behind. When he looked at Richard lying on the floor, the butler's face paled. Even though Conrad killed Frederick, Levi knew he did it to protect Gretta. Levi would do all he could to make sure the butler had the best lawyer so he wouldn't end up hanging from the end of a rope for murder. Maybe the judge would allow Conrad to be in Levi's custody until he worked off his penance.

"Conrad," Levi said. "Go fetch the sheriff. We just found the jewel thief."

The butler nodded and ran out of the room. Levi breathed easier now. At least he had fulfilled his promise and protected both Gretta and her brother.

"Charles?" she said, touching his arm. "Uncle Reginald went to Heaven tonight."

Charles glared at Richard. "Was this man the reason?"

"No," she said softly. "It was Uncle Reginald's time to go."

Tears filled Charles' eyes and he nodded. "Then I suppose that while Conrad is fetching the sheriff, I should fetch the coroner."

She nodded. "That is probably wise."

Charles kissed his sister's forehead. "Our uncle is out of pain now."

"I know," she answered brokenly.

Charles smiled at Levi. "And thank you so much for your help. You'll never know how much we appreciate it."

"Um, Charles?" Gretta said, gaining her brother's attention. "You will be the first to know, but... Levi and I are engaged."

Charles' eyes widened in surprise, and he let out a loud laugh, clamping his hand on Levi's shoulder.

"Etta, you picked a fine man indeed."

Levi grinned. He was happy to be joining a family who respected him, and one he would get along with.

She moved away from her brother and wrapped her arms around Levi. "He is the best man I know."

Levi's heart melted. If he didn't love her already, he definitely loved her now, but his love grew for her with each minute.

EPILOGUE

Levi gazed at his wonderful bride. He never thought he could be this happy, but he was very glad that he had been wrong. If Gretta pleased him this much now, he was sure the rest of their married life would be pure bliss.

She looked so very lovely in her white wedding gown. Her sleeves were bell-shaped, and her bodice was square cut, showing a hint of her full bosom. Silver ribbons were sewn around the hem and the edges of her sleeves and neckline, as well as the matching ribbon wound in her loose bun sitting high on the back of her head. Tendrils hung around her ears. But it was her brilliant smile that made her the most beautiful woman he had ever seen. He loved staring at her, and thankfully, she acted like she didn't mind at all.

After they had exchanged vows and rings, and shared a kiss as husband and wife, their guests came up to greet them. There was a picnic of refreshments displayed on tables in the church's yard. All of Gretta's servants were there, and many of his Pinkerton friends.

Levi and Gretta waited a month after Uncle Reginald's funeral to get married. Thankfully, she didn't want to wait for the customary grieving period of six months before marrying Levi. He wasn't sure he was patient enough to withstand the separation. He was happy that their friends didn't seem to mind, either.

Levi and Gretta received their guests, but he was anxious for it to all be over so that he could take his bride home and make her his wife in the Biblical sense. And from the gleam in her pretty eyes when she looked at him, he thought she shared his anxiousness.

A tall, slender, middle-aged man, professionally dressed, walked up to them, and removed his hat. He bowed to Gretta.

"Allow me to wish you well with your marriage," the man said. "I dropped something off at the manor last night, but I'm not certain if you received it."

Gretta narrowed her eyes. "What was it you dropped off?"

"It was your uncle's last will and testament."

She gasped. "Uncle Reginald's will?"

The man nodded. "When you return from your honeymoon, you can make an appointment with me, and I'll go over it with you."

"All right, I can do that." Gretta paused. "Can you tell me briefly what was in the will?"

The man's smile stretched across his face. "As you probably know, your uncle was wealthy. He split his money between you and your brother. In order for you to obtain the funds, both you and Mr. Ramsay will have to sign some documents."

Shocked, Levi could do nothing but stare at his wife. He couldn't possibly have heard correctly. Gretta was wealthy now?

"Oh, my." She placed a hand on her bosom as though she struggled to catch her breath. "Mr. Hamlin, this is wonderful news. I didn't realize my uncle had done that."

The lawyer nodded. "Congratulations to you both on your wedding. I was more than happy to give you such wonderful news on this special day."

Levi shook himself out of the stupor the news had put him in, and quickly shook the lawyer's hand. After the man walked away, Gretta slid an arm around Levi's waist and peered up into his eyes.

"Can you believe it?"

"No. I'm still trying to process the news." He chuckled. "But you know I would love and cherish you even if we are poor and homeless, right?"

She nodded. "Of course."

Someone stood in front of him, clearing his throat. Levi tore his attention from his wife and rested it on his friend, Harrison

Gretta's Gamble

Holt. As he opened his mouth to greet his friend, he also noticed the man and woman standing behind Harrison. Another jolt of surprise shook through Levi. What was Alexa Moore and her husband doing here?

"Thank you for coming, Mr. Holt," Gretta said sweetly. "It is good to see you again."

Harrison took her hand and kissed her knuckles. Levi was glad that jealousy didn't eat at him this time. Still, he didn't know what to say. He hadn't expected to see the woman he thought he had loved with her husband at *his* wedding, even if Levi had worked briefly with Ash Hawkins, he certainly hadn't invited them to his wedding.

Levi focused on his friend, who looked at him with a knowing grin. Inwardly, he groaned. Now he knew why Harrison was here, and why he felt that Alexa had to come as well. *The wager.* Still stinging from Alexa's rejection, Levi had made a bet with his friends to give up something he treasured, which was his grandmother's pearl necklace. If the friend lost the bet, they would forfeit their possession to the person who ruined their life. In Levi's case, it would go to Alexa.

"I hope you don't mind that I showed up unannounced," Harrison said.

Levi shook his head. "Nonsense. You are my friend and have every right to celebrate this glorious day with me and my bride."

Harrison stepped closer. "Do you remember our wager?"

Levi groaned again. He didn't want Gretta knowing, but he also didn't want to keep secrets from her any longer.

"How could I forget?" Levi replied. Gretta's confused expression let him know he had better do some quick explaining. "You see, my love, almost six months ago, my childhood friends and I made a bet that none of us would marry. If we did, we would give up something that was very special to us. I wagered the pearl necklace from my grandmother that she wanted me to give to my bride." He switched his focus to Harrison. "And I'll gladly hand that over, because Gretta's love is more important to me than anything."

Harrison scratched his clean-shaven chin. "And you were going to forfeit the necklace to the person who you thought had ruined your life."

Levi nodded. "I remember, and I will do that once I return from my honeymoon."

Harrison stepped aside and motioned toward Alexa. "You remember Mr. and Mrs. Hawkins, correct?"

Levi's stomach twisted. How could he nicely explain to Gretta why Alexa was here? His wedding was supposed to be a joyous occasion, so why was Harrison trying to ruin it for him?

Alexa smiled and stepped up to Gretta, reaching out her hand to shake. His wife smiled and shook the woman's hand.

"Allow me to introduce myself before Levi says something wrong." Alexa winked. "I knew your husband when he lived in Colorado. At the time, I thought I wanted to be a Pinkerton agent, and Levi was kind enough to give me some advice. However, I made him think I had feelings for him, when I was secretly falling in love with this man." She motioned toward Ash, who chuckled. "Anyway, I thought I had ruined Levi's life, which is why he moved to New York City. But I'm happy to see, God has a plan for everyone. If Levi hadn't moved back here, he would have never met and fallen in love with you."

Gretta beamed and leaned against Levi. "Indeed. God has a plan for us all."

"And so," Alexa continued as she switched her focus to Harrison, "because I now realize I hadn't ruined Levi's life, I will not accept his grandmother's pearl necklace." She met Levi's stare. "Your grandmother intended it to go to your bride, which is where it needs to be."

A gush of relieved air sprang from Levi's throat. He wanted to hug Alexa in thanks for her sweet explanation, but more than that, he wanted to give the necklace to Gretta now. If only he had it on him.

He took his bride in his embrace and gazed into her dreamy eyes. "Alexa is right. God knew *you* were the woman I should give my heart to, and I will be eternally grateful I was put into your path and that you gave me a second chance at love."

Gretta's Gamble

Gretta sighed and cupped his cheek. "I love you, Levi Montgomery."

"And I love you."

Not caring that they had people watching, he bent and gave his wife a kiss, keeping it simple but tender. Perhaps his day hadn't been ruined by his friend. But what mattered the most was that he and Gretta would start their new lives together, and from this day forward, nothing—and no one—would stand in their way of true happiness.

THE END

Other published stories by Marie Higgins

https://www.authormariehiggins.com/books

Other published stories by Stacey Haynes

https://www.amazon.com/Stacey-Haynes/e/B088NTQQPJ

Join Marie's newsletter and add to your reading collection -

https://www.authormariehiggins.com/newsletter

MARIE'S BIO

Marie Higgins is a best-selling, multi-published author of Christian and sweet romance novels; from refined bad-boy heroes who make your heart melt to the feisty heroines who somehow manage to love them regardless of their faults. She's been with a Christian publisher since 2010. Between those and her others, she's published over 100 heartwarming, on-the-edge-of-your-seat stories and broadened her readership by writing mystery/suspense, humor, time-travel, paranormal, along with her love for historical romances. Her readers have dubbed her "Queen of Tease", because of all her twists and turns and unexpected endings.

Visit her website to discover more about her – https://authormariehiggins.com

STACEY'S BIO

Stacey Haynes is an award-winning, and best-selling author. She has always enjoyed reading and writing romance stories beginning with her first story in 6th grade. Her dream has always been to have one of her books published, and now she has several, including a poem about her most disliked food, Peas!

She won her first writing contest when she and her sister, Marie, entered their story The Magic of a Billionaire into an online writing contest on www.ajoara.com – and their story won 1st place!

She considers herself a hopeless romantic and tries to find the best in others. She loves to write in her spare time to relax after a hard day at work.

Stacey lives in Utah with her wonderful husband and three adorable children. She hopes to have more books published in her lifetime.

You can follow her adventures on Facebook – http://www.facebook.com/StaceyHaynes
https://www.facebook.com/Stacey-Haynes-Author-110345070332647

Instagram – https://www.instagram.com/Staceybuns1969/

Bookbub – https://www.bookbub.com/authors/stacey-haynes

Made in the USA
Coppell, TX
19 September 2023